St

ØFC 13

ØGF5

ØGR

THE KILLER THING

Books by Kate Wilhelm

THE KILLER THING

THE NEVERMORE AFFAIR

MORE BITTER THAN DEATH

THE MILE LONG SPACESHIP

(In Collaboration with Theodore L. Thomas)

THE CLONE

KATE WILHELM

The Killer Thing

1967

Doubleday & Company, Inc., Garden City, New York

*All of the characters in this book
are fictitious, and any resemblance
to actual persons, living or dead,
is purely coincidental.*

Library of Congress Catalog Card Number 66–20972
Copyright © 1967 by Kate Wilhelm
All Rights Reserved
Printed in the United States of America
First Edition

This book is dedicated to the following with my warmest appreciation: Ted Thomas and Gordy Dickson, who made suggestions; John Brunner, for invaluable advice; and A. J. Budrys. Thanks, fellows.

THE KILLER THING

One

There was the desert, glittering white sand that shifted like talcum when touched, cottony white sky, a quarter of it glaring with the white heat of the sun. There was no wind, no movement anywhere; not a grain of the powdery sand stirred. It looked like a blanket of white wool interwoven with silver threads in a random pattern, a blanket tossed down carelessly so that it rippled in smooth hills, all rising diagonally in a series. The cover stretched endlessly, hiding the rocky land under it from the gaze of the man, and where his vision failed, the bleached wool merged with the white cotton and the world was enclosed, as if he stood on the inside of a flattened sphere. Behind him, and in the distance between him and the desert, naked rocks thrust from the burned ground, as barren as the view before him.

The rocks were basalts, granites, quartzites. Nothing as soft and weather vulnerable as sandstone existed above ground surface, but no weather stirred the air now, no wind blew. It would blow later, when the sun started to sink and the ground radiated away some of the heat load of the long day; it would blow for five or six hours then, exchanging heat for cool air, thin columns of tornadolike wind rising from the superheated ground to the high, thin atmosphere, to fall back through masses of hot air, whirling them about, starting new funnels. With the dawn the winds would have spent themselves, having established some sort of uneasy equilibrium; the sun rise would start them again, shafts of heat stirring the night-cooled air more and more violently until the atmosphere was hot, the ground hotter, and the tumultuous wind became a gentle, steady breeze that died to nothing, as if the wind were anxious to amend the damage inflicted during the night, smooth back the tortured sands that had been whipped and tossed, and leave them in graceful rows of softly rounded dunes.

The man knew he could not remain that far from his base very long; his need to get away from it had been overpowering, however, and today he had given in to the need. He lifted his pack, bending under its weight, his lungs and heart straining with the added burden, and he started to retrace his steps to his camp, keeping always in the shadows of the rocks. He was a big man, over six feet tall, well muscled, and young at thirty-two, but the air was thin. He did not have the added burden of oxygen tanks on this planet, but as his lungs strained for air he wondered if it wouldn't be worth carrying them. Then he remembered they were empty. His suit was highly reflective, white, topped with a helmet that was wired and equipped to do things he couldn't do without. He had turned up the audio so that, if the killer robot moved within three miles of him, he would be able to hear it. And he had adjusted the transparent face piece so that he could look out at the glaring world without risking "snow blindness." In doing this he had cut down his visual field; he could not see the depths of the shadows cast by the grotesquely shaped rocks, and he could not see as far as his eyes unaided would have been able to, but neither would he go blind. As far as the killer robot was concerned, it would make no difference if he were blind or not.

His camp was the dinghy that had brought him from his ship, now in stationary orbit, invisible through the glare of the sun, but showing as a pearl drop of light late in the day when the sun started its descent. The dinghy was wedged between two mammoth columns of basalt three miles away. Every day he changed his camp, skimming the dinghy as

close to the surface of the planet as he could, not settling
for a new location less than fifty miles from the last. He had
fuel remaining to move only three more times, reserving
enough to take him back to the orbiting ship. The killer
robot, obviously gravely damaged, was advancing at the
rate of only five miles an hour, but even that reduced speed
was much faster than the man, struggling against both heat
and thin atmosphere, could travel by foot.

He stopped in his march and listened. Something had
clanged against a rock to his left. He flattened himself
against the rock and didn't move for the next ten minutes;
there was no further sound. Cautiously then he moved away
from the rock, around it, into the shadow of the next one.
An energy beam cut through the granite above him, turning
it cherry red, then white, and finally vaporizing it. The man
clung to his base. He was sheltered from a direct line of fire,
surrounded as he was by the shafts that remained of ancient
hills and mountains. Maybe the thing was trying to crush
him with falling rocks. . . .

No! He closed his eyes then, too tight, feeling pain in
them.

It can't do anything that requires imagination, remember
that, Trace. It's got a computer for a brain. It's been programmed to kill with the laser, and the fusion shells, and
that's all.

You were wrong, boy! Didn't you hear me telling you it
blinked out? Just like that, out! Gone! It's got something
new, boy, a screen it can hide behind.

The voice had been there, in his ears, but it was gone
now; everything was gone. The silence was complete, ex-
cluded even his own breathing and heart beat. *How used
to hearing ourselves we get. I miss it.* It couldn't move so
quietly that he wouldn't hear it, even if he never saw it

again. Not with its metal over the bare rocks, not with the
radioactive trail it left behind it. The radiation alarm hadn't
sounded this time. Was the thing learning to stalk him, keeping the dense, radiation-damping rocks between itself and
the man it hunted?

Two miles was its limit of fire; it must have been waiting
quietly for him to blunder within that range. That meant it
had to be somewhere even with him, or in front of him. . . .
He had heard it to his left; he was certain now that that was
what he had heard, some slight shifting it made preparatory
to firing. He began to squirm along the ground to his right,
keeping close to the base of the rocks, dragging his pack after
him. It fired once more, the beam falling short, still playing
around the column he had left. After he had gone a quarter
of a mile, he got to his feet cautiously at the foot of a basalt
group that was sixty feet across and twice as high. His camp
was still thirty minutes away. He wondered if the thing had
found it. He shouldn't have risked leaving it, adding to the
original mistake by not taking into account his own weakness, the enervating effects of too much sun, too little
oxygen. But the killer robot shouldn't have followed him this
far so soon, either. Was it learning to cope with the uneven
ground? Was it working on repairing its speed control?

He stopped his thoughts and listened instead to the
voices:

The shell hit us, Trace, knocked out the secondary control
room.

Stan, Morris . . . ?

They're all dead. You still have a fix on it?

Yeah, still closing, but pressure is going fast. We'll have to
abandon . . .

What's it doing now?

Our hit must have bollixed the controls; it's starting to
spin.

They watched the ship they had chased for over three months, fixed on it so that it couldn't shake them, entering warp sector after sector on its tail, always closing in, but not close enough to shoot it down, and now they knew that they had closed the gap. Trace's fingers started toward the fire control and then drew back. A red light was flashing belligerently, and three green lights had flicked off. He turned to Duncan. Ready the dinghy.

It's ready. It's still firing. Looks like a random pattern.

The ship tumbled end over end, toward the planet, and every time it was in a position to fire the fusion shells, its automatic system fired a barrage. The patrol ship, limping now with its rear section gone, its protective screen damaged and ineffective, couldn't maneuver, and aboard her the men could only wait.

It's going to fire every damn shell in the ship.

Wouldn't you?

They couldn't fire back, and they couldn't change position except by using the main braking rockets, which were still green in the major control panel. The lights over the maneuvering controls had gone out with the hit. Two more lights started to blink red and the ship shuddered once. There was an acrid smell of smoldering insulation.

We have to damp it. Pressure going faster. Check pressure suits.

Okay.

We'll put her in stationary orbit and turn everything off. Communications gone. Didn't get to finish the message . . . not enough oxygen to wait up here for a rescue. Looks like we sit it out planet-side. Good thing we got our fix off before the hit.

The ship shuddered again and a whole row of lights flashed red. A second hit . . .

Trace shook his head violently, clearing away the distant yet distinct voices, forcing out the scenes that played whenever he forgot to look away. He stumbled on toward the

dinghy, his legs aching with his exertion, his whole body
sagging now, exhausted by the heat and the effort of getting
enough oxygen from the thin air on this planet. Before he
approached the dinghy, he patrolled a circle around it, looking for tracks of the robot, his radiation detector turned on
high, because the thing had got hot along with its ship, and
it was still radiating furiously. No radiation escaped its
screen, but the ground it touched got hot. Searching for
tracks was automatic, done without any real hope of finding
any in the sand that lay between the rocks. The few times
he had found visible tracks had only added to his bewilder-
ment, until he realized the robot had several different means
of travel; it had wheels, and treads, and something else—
spherical, something that left one broad three-foot swath of
crushed rocks and packed sand behind it. Trace refused to
allow himself to think what it would be like if it had been
able to regain its ability to travel as fast as the treads indicated it should. Tracks usually registered only through the
clicking voice of the radiation detector. This time it remained quiet.

The thing hadn't been there. The area was clean. Trace
went directly to the dinghy and locked himself in. Before
he removed his helmet, he adjusted the detectors inside
the small craft, and then he undressed. The temperature
inside the dinghy was 108, almost fifteen degrees cooler than
outside, and although Trace was perspiring profusely, the
dried air took the moisture as it formed. His skin felt crusty
with salt and dirt. The dinghy was a two seater, the two
reclining seats side by side, a foot apart before the abbre-
viated control panel. There was only room enough behind
the seats for the emergency stores needed by a two-man
scout team—medical supplies, emergency rations, lights, and
the all-weather suits. There had been extra oxygen tanks, but
Trace had tossed them out to make more room after he had
exhausted them. When the dinghy had landed it was with

a hole he could put his fist through, and with Duncan unconscious, his chest smashed by a meteorite.

Don't do it, Trace. You'll need it.

Duncan's whisper. His voice was still in the dinghy, as if it had penetrated every wall to seep out slowly over the coming weeks, a little at a time, always whispering.

The plastic Trace had used for his oxygen tent was still draped over the right-hand seat, Duncan's seat, and it gleamed black-red where it touched the cushion and was held to it by static electricity.

Trace ate sparingly, not regretful of the need to conserve his stocks. The heat took his sweat, his appetite, his energy. He wished the dinghy had a water converter, and thought longingly of the disabled converter on the mother ship hanging over the world of sand and rocks.

After he ate, there was nothing to do. He would move soon, but not yet, not until the thing got closer, not until it was nearly nighttime, so the robot wouldn't track him down during the long night and find him asleep. It moved toward him unceasingly now that there were only the two of them, and the attack of that noon had been the fourth one so far in the three-week-old hunt. Another week and a half to go before Trace could expect relief, another week and a half of playing hide and seek with the killer robot. He stared at the screen that showed his own trail, and there was nothing but the rocks and the sand. The shadows were growing now, and soon he would be in a nightmare world of black monoliths that rose dizzily, crookedly into the white sky, and black lines that striped the white sand among the feet of the rocks. This was the bad time—waiting for the wind when the stripes were obscured by blowing sand—the silent, unmoving time of the long shadows that were nowhere gray, but were unyielding black against white.

Duncan's whisper came to him again, and he cocked his head to listen.

It can't get off the planet now, Trace, but no one else knows it's here. You have to stay alive and tell them, Trace. There's no one else now. The message didn't get through in time, cut off after the fix was reported. That's all they know. They'll find the ship up there, and they'll search for the dinghy, but they won't be looking for the killer. Tell them, Trace. Tell them.

"Sure, Duncan," Trace said out loud, in a normal conversational tone, looking about for him. He shook himself and stood up, fear standing out in the form of small beads of cold sweat about his mouth and nose. He made coffee then and drank it black and hot, and only once looked at the striped world showing itself on the screen.

It was being alone that made it bad, he told himself, sipping a second cup of coffee. He couldn't remember ever being alone before in his life. The crews of the patrol were always six or eight men, and the dinghies carried two or more. No one went out in space alone, and when your partner slept, you could still hear his breathing. Even if you couldn't hear him, you always knew he was there. It made a difference, knowing another man was there. He caught himself listening too hard, and he pulled out the log he had been keeping and started to fill it in for that day. His mind wandered from it again and again; in the end he wrote nothing. He re-examined his calculations instead.

He had enough oxygen to last four days on the ship in orbit after he left the planet, and he had enough fuel to move 150 miles, a thirty-hour trip for the robot. Even counting the time it would take for the robot to locate him after the moves, he had no more than forty hours of comparative safety remaining to him on the ground. He could not leave the planet for at least a week. . . . So far he had been lucky, had dared remain after he knew his location had been spotted by the thing's sensors. He had been able to rely on his sound system to warn him when the thing was getting near enough to fire. The robot always found him. No matter what damage the hit they had scored on it or the crash landing had done, its sensors were working well enough for it to keep finding him. He had no way of knowing what functions had been repaired, had no way of knowing what functions had been built into it. One by one, as they were manifested, he wrote them down, but each new ability was a surprise and a threat.

He didn't dare leave the planet any sooner than he had to, because the robot could repair its own dinghy. He had caught it busy at the repair job the first day of their enforced stay on the planet.

Standing high on a ridge cut out on a basalt cliff, he had seen the thing for the first time. It was ten feet high, with a barrel-like chest and retractable waldoes then wielding tools. The dinghy had left the crippled, falling ship like a shot, plunging straight down towards the planet, glowing red then white as it plummeted. Trace and Duncan had watched it, certain that the robot killer had burned up with it. They didn't see it land, and not until Trace saw the metal monster repairing it did he consider that the robot might have survived such a landing. It had sensed him before he was close enough to fire at it with the small hand gun he carried, and the robot had blinked out. A second later the dinghy was gone too. Somehow the robot had brought the little dinghy to ground without an explosion, and it was repairing the craft. It had already made operational a force field that was new, that curved light and caused invisibility.

Watching it before it blinked out, Trace had wondered at the reports claiming invulnerability for the machine, but then, knowing it was there, that it had a laser that could

vaporize metal and rocks in half a minute or less, he had
felt fear. He had run. Three weeks later, he was still running.

He was listening again, and this time there was an external
sound; the small craft was being pelted with sand, and the
wind was starting to whistle among the rocks. A dismal,
faint sound now, it would howl and screech and scream
maniacally later. It was time to leave this spot for another,
fifty miles away. He took his seat at the controls; just
before he left the ground he heard the radiation detector
start warning him in a staccato voice. It was coming.

I can't find the dinghy. . . . It's deflecting the radiation
downward, into the ground. None of it's escaping. . . .
Destroy the dinghy and then hide, Trace. No other way.
Can't find it.
Keep it too busy to go back and fix the dinghy. Keep it
after you, too busy to go back. . . .

Two

Trace took off then, feeling the shiver that passed through the small lifeboat when it left the ground and was hit by the wind that already was picking up strength away from the sheltering bases of the mountains. He flew with the wind pushing behind him, heading the dinghy east, straight out over the desert, away from the metal monster. The sun was going down behind him, lengthening to slivers the pointed shadows that lay across the rippled sand. Then the mountain shadows were gone and nothing but the sand was there. In the distance it seemed on fire, a ground-hugging, seething, molten lava lake ready to erupt to the sky in open flames. He looked behind him and could see the black fingers of mountains against the sky that was turning violet, like a rare, icy orchid being ripped with the black witches' claws. Away from the mountains, in the east, the sky was becoming black, with night, with sand being raised from the desert floor. He flew twenty-five miles away from the mountains, and then headed north again, knowing he needed the bony lap shelter offered by the ravaged framework of the mountains. Once, days ago, he had tried to hide on the desert, and had lost one entire day in digging the little craft out from the hill of sand that had covered it overnight.

When he landed again, he had covered only fifteen miles in a straight line from the old camp, but maybe it would follow him out on the sands this time. When he could, he moved only minutes before the winds made moving impossible, always hoping the effects of the moving sand under

the tornadolike wind would erase his trail. The last ten or
fifteen miles he always hugged the bones of the mountains,
hoping to damp his trail, hoping their mass would absorb his
heat and noise, and whatever else it was that brought the
robot to his new camp each day.

He chose his site carefully despite the wind gusts of fifty
miles an hour, and the darkness that was enveloping the
landscape. His craft was under a three-hundred-foot-high
shelf that was being eaten out from below, leaving an over-
hang of forty feet.

Ain't exactly Joyland, is it, Trace?

Lousy luck, that's all. Just that one ridge we saw, that and
sand. . . .

Yeah. Well, six hundred miles of bare bones to play around
for the next couple of weeks. We might get in some pros-
pecting. . . .

Watch out, Duncan! Object seven o'clock!

Very carefully Trace turned off the controls, forcing the
voices away, refusing to go through it again. With the immediate need of action gone, he felt drained, and his exhaustion from the heat and the strenuous walk flooded him.
He touched the stud that leveled out the seat into a bed, and
he stretched out, his hands behind his head, eyes closed. It's
the end of this particular trail, he thought, drifting. From
out on the desert he had seen that the mountains ended
only a few miles beyond his camp. At this point the range
was less than twenty miles wide, too narrow to hide in,
certainly. He shouldn't have tried that last maneuver. But
perhaps this one time it would do something wrong. . . .

A wry smile twisted his lips, although his eyes remained
closed.

It can do no wrong, unless wrong has been programmed into
it. It's a logic box. Nothing but a logic box. It can do only

what it's been programmed to do, and that's it. If right and wrong are related in any way to logic and illogic, then it can do no wrong. It has been given a finite number of facts, and a finite number of propositions expressing relationships between those facts. It cannot question the validity of what it has been given, it can only act on those facts and relationships. And heaven help me, because I can question and doubt and make judgment mistakes. . . .

The wind howled, and tornadoes formed and lifted rocks, sand, boulders, sent them flying and crashing into the mountains. Immense slabs of granite were raised, ground together, and finally deposited as coarse sand that would be rubbed down finer and finer until it was like polishing powder.

How did it manage to dodge them? Did it keep to the lee side of the mountains always? Did it walk among shadows where the wind whistled past but did not enter? Trace drifted; one muscle at a time, it seemed, jerked and relaxed, and then his hands slid out from under his head, one of them resting on his chest, the other dangling from the reclining seat, not quite touching the floor.

The bony, black fingers reaching for the sky curled in on themselves and crept along the ground, joining where they met other fingers, forming a black wall that was impenetrable. From the black forward line of the wall, new fingers probed tentatively, feeling their way around rocks, over boulders, dragging the wall after them, and the wall was getting closer and closer to him. He could not move as it formed, but suddenly was freed, and then he darted about crazily, looking for an opening in the wall, being forced backward, step by step, until he knew there was nothing behind him but a chasm, and he could back up no farther. Again he froze, his eyes compelled to watch the progress of the wall.

It was there in the shadows. He could feel it as a horror too great to bear alone. If only someone would come along and open the wall for him. They would say nothing was there, nothing but the shadows; only he knew better. He knew it was there. It existed although he could not see it; when it moved he felt a tug; when he moved, he could feel it changing direction, an answering tug. It was in the shadows, and it was growing larger, filling in the shadows, spreading to fill every bend and curve and crack. His eyes deceived him, but his mind knew it was there. He could even understand its method now, its purpose. With the helpful fingers of the shadows to reach out and touch him, hold him until the thing got nearer, the thing would get him. He couldn't back up. He could only wait. The fingers crept from the darkness, twisting, feeling their blind way along the ground, and they grew nearer and nearer to where he crouched. He watched them, unable even to breathe, and felt the thing behind the fingers.

He was too tired to run again, the chasm was too deep for him to jump over. He wanted to weep and couldn't. The wall moved and one of the fingers was only inches away from his legs. He shivered. If only he knew what was in the chasm behind him it wouldn't be so bad. Or if he knew where the other edge of the crevice was, perhaps he could still jump across it. He was too tired to make the effort it would take to turn and look. All his life he had been running from it and now it was there, inches away from his legs. Always running away, never able to stop and look at it, no name, no shape, no reason for being, but it was there, coming closer and closer. And he was afraid. His shivering increased and he couldn't stop that either. The shadow touched his leg suddenly and he shrieked, "Duncan! Help me!"

His voice awakened him. The nightmare was gone, leaving nothing but the memory of the fear that had knotted his stomach. He was shivering. He got up and checked his dinghy then; it had come through the windstorm without damage, and now the wind was gone, the night completely still. The dinghy was fifteen feet long, tapering from nine feet at its widest point to a blunt tail. The two seat-beds were over the engines and the front was filled with controls. There were circular windows of quartz over the seats; two more, smaller, over the storage units behind the seats. All the windows were covered, protected from the windstorms. The hatch was an oval, five feet high, three feet wide, but the entire rear section of the little boat could be opened in order to take on a stretcher or a man in full in-space pressure suit.

The robot must have entered its own dinghy that way, it must have ripped out the seats to get to the controls. . . .

He stepped outside, listening, feeling the cold night air on his skin, unwilling to return to sleep right away, despite the fact that he felt as tired as he had when he first lay down. He had slept four hours at the most, not enough to make up for the unaccustomed exercise of the day before, or the unending tension.

It was very dark on the planet, with only the pale indifferent starlight above. The mountain peaks were merely darker blobs against a dark star-pricked sky. The stars shone steadily, looking very far away and unreachable. He felt alone in the universe as he stared up at the unfamiliar sky.

There are worlds out there, he told himself, not knowing if he thought the words or said them. Worlds where ships are making regular trade runs, where fleets are maneuvering, buildings going up, wars going on, worlds where men are finding new things for the first time. Any of them might look up and feel alone. It isn't just me. Somewhere in warp sector a fleet ship is flashing near the speed of light, coming for me. I'm not really alone, not for long.

Damn him! Why hadn't Duncan stayed alive? Why hadn't they sent two ships after the metal monster? He went back inside, thoroughly chilled, still unwilling to face again the dream that had wakened him. He pulled out his space charts, wondering how far along the relief ship was by then. It should be in orbit in seven or eight days, ten at the most.

He looked at the familiar worlds: Earth, Venus, Mars— the original World Group, won through hard fighting. First had come the feeble colonies on Mars, and in another fifteen years those on Venus. Then came a hiatus of nearly one hundred years, during which time the colonies grew, became powerful, waged war with Earth, and finally formed the World Group Government. Only then had come the nearer stars and their planets, taken one by one, painfully, with losses on both sides that none cared to think about any more. Seven Class A planets had been found so far, seven major planets with highly developed civilizations, with "common stock" human beings, and the seven had fought off the armies of the World Group. But they had taken and held them, all of them, and finally the seven had surrendered; now they were practically equal partners.

Trace didn't even know how many minor planets had been found, although it was one of the first lessons taught in astropolitics. The numbers changed from week to week almost. Like an amoeba the powers had grown—the Earth splintering off a human segment to make the Mars Colony, to settle Venus, then the three rejoining, bigger, stronger than ever. After that the growth had been faster and faster, until now when a pseudopod reached out and claimed a new world for the parent body, there was little excitement. The organism had grown very large, and was reaching out in every direction, hungry for new worlds, impregnable, invulnerable now, seizing what it touched, incorporating all that fell before it.

This world would be added to the total, he knew, another minor planet, and he would receive a bonus. A team would be sent here to investigate its possibilities; if it had anything of value on it, the proper office of the government would be informed. In due time the proper group of people would be dispatched to take the new wealth back to the government. Mining camps might spring up on a world such as this one. Water would be made from the materials of the planet itself, the atmosphere doctored until it was more amenable for humans, who would clean it of everything needed, or wanted, on the other worlds.

If a planet was inhabited when found, the pattern changed but little. Sometimes the natives resisted the efforts to take from their world the spoils of exploration, but their resistance never lasted long. Sometimes they were eager for trade with extraterrestrials. It mattered little in the end. Minor planet, major planet, it mattered little.

As Trace stared at the tiny worlds depicted on the charts, they started to spin before his face, as if whirling in orbit, and he pushed the charts back into their rack. He felt lightheaded with fatigue when he crept back into his seat-bed. It would have helped if this world had a better atmosphere, he thought. It was like trying to live on a mountain peak after being used to the thick heady air of the valleys.

He heard the sand then, its shiftings like whispers, too faint to make out the words, but a steady rising and falling sound of distant voices speaking with hushed tones. He listened harder. He knew it was the sand, settling now after the wind finished with it. The wind piled the sands high against rocks, against the dinghy, and after the winds left, the sand rested awhile and then started shifting, seeking a comfortable balance with gravity once more. Some of it was running from the top of the little lifeboat, growing louder at

a point just over his left shoulder, then fading again, voices
rising and falling in conversation. . . .

We saw the thing, Trace, don't you remember? After the
space fight in Sector Thirteen, near Ramses. . . .
Yeah. We both got passes—three days on Ramses.
The screen was nicked a little, needed fixing. Wasn't that
it? Anyway, we went to the mine, remember where Dr.
what's-his-name was fooling around with the mining robots.
You said you were going to report the thing. Did you, Trace?
I never did ask you if you did.
I reported it, Duncan.

He remembered, in his dream, seeing the thing in Dr.
Vianti's laboratory. It had stood over eight feet tall, on
treads, with a domelike top that could be swiveled. The
others were good only for mining, but this one, the one the
doctor was working with, it could do almost anything.

It's almost as if you're the proud father, Trace. That nutty
doctor wouldn't have told anyone about it. He'd still be back
there changing it, talking to it like a baby, or a pet dog, or
something, everything as innocent as nursery school. You're
its father, Trace. How about that?

Ramses. He remembered Ramses.

Three

"Welcome to Ramses, land of little people, big drinks, and open mines! The women are small, but brother, watch out, they do know what they are doing!" Lo Ti chanted, glancing through a guidebook he had picked up at the spaceport. "Any of you ever been to Ramses before?" He was a second lieutenant, of Korean descent.

Trace and Duncan shook their heads with the others. Trace stretched out full length in a reclining seat in the railed carrier that had been sent to transport the fleet from the spaceport to the nearest city. It was a pleasant feeling, being back on ground again after six months in space, four of them in battle.

"For your edification, gentlemen, may I enlighten you?" Lo Ti grinned, not looking to see the suffering expressions the other men assumed at his words. Someone moaned, "Cork him!" Another muttered, "Let's toss him out!" Lo Ti ignored them.

"Ramses, admitted to the World Group Government as a protectorate in 2158. Population of one billion, seventeen million. Principal exports, platinum, magnesium, peridots, and related minerals. Humanoids, sub-class C, averaging five feet two inches for the males, four feet six inches for the females of the species. State of technology comparable to Earth in year 1975, sans space travel . . ."

From the other end of the carrier a chant began that gradually picked up voices, finally drowning out the grin-

ning second lieutenant, whose lips continued to move as he
read from the guidebook.

> Oh, we've seen girls
> Didn't look like girls,
> Had to ask before you'd know 'em.
> They don't have girls
> Like they make the girls
> Back where we call ho-em!

There was much laughter, and someone started another
of the fleet songs:

> With a roar and a flame
> I'm well in the game
> With a pain that scrambles my brain.
> A ton on my chest,
> I'm part of the best
> God-damned race to ever hit space!
>
> They bow when we come;
> They know where we're from.
> On their knees they're trying to please.
> When the air is okay,
> And the girls built that way,
> In the end we'll make only a friend.

The song went on for six more verses, each verse less in-
hibited than the last, and Duncan and Trace bellowed out
the words with the others. Trace was grinning broadly when
the bawdy song ended, and the carrier slowed down to
follow winding city streets. He turned to look about.

The carrier was on tracks that were six feet above ground
level, rising to cross roads and buildings now and then, falling to skim over the surface by inches of clearance, and then
rising again. The buildings were of translucent green stone
for the most part, with dark polished trim and jade-green

inlays in geometric patterns. The roofs were white, very clean and sparkling. The same shades of green, ranging from pale gray-green, through emerald, to black-green, were everywhere: in the streets, sidewalks, buildings, contrasted with the dazzling white, and with brilliant complementary colors in unexpected places. There were orange and red umbrellas over canary-yellow tables along the sidewalks, awnings with red swirls on white, rows and rows of deep-purple flowers in white planters, trees with gray and white leaves.

People were everywhere. They looked like children masquerading as adults. The women were petite, graceful, with long flowing hair and tiny hands and feet. They were from four feet to not quite five feet in height, and were dressed in pastel tunics that were fastened at the shoulders with jade and peridot clasps. Their hair was agleam with the green ornaments; pendant earrings swung as they walked. The men wore longer tunics that were as simple as the women's, but were white and black, or gray. They wore hip pouches held in place by wide metallic belts. Their heads as well as their faces were clean shaven.

"Nice, isn't it?" Duncan said, at Trace's side.

He was as tall as Trace, and, at twenty-three, three years younger. Both were second lieutenants. His black eyes were shining with the excitement of leave after four months' running battle with the fleet dispatched by Mellic. "You have any plans for the duration?" he asked.

They had come to a larger shopping area, where stores were open to the warm air and sunshine, and goods were spread out to be seen and handled.

"No," Trace said. "You?"

"Shopping first, for my sisters. I promised them something from each world I get to see, you know. They're dopes, think all I have to do is shop for gewgaws for them." He looked pleased at the thought.

Trace grinned at him. "Okay, we shop and sight-see. How about taking a look at the mines?"

"Yeah, that's great."

They roamed the streets, laughing at the musical tones of incomprehension voiced by the natives when they tried to explain what they wanted. They lunched in a sidewalk cafe where they ate food they couldn't identify and drank a pale-green, milky liqueur that made their heads swim pleasantly. Somewhere along the way they picked up two girls, each of them under four and a half feet, looking more like dolls than like women. The one who linked her arm through Trace's said her name was Fez. She spoke in broken English; her eyes were like immense green lakes, flecked with golden-brown dots. Later that night the girls took them to a hotel where the furnishings were golden and white silks and soft candlewood, and the four of them bathed and swam in their own pool with a center fountain of translucent olivine rock.

Fez was very beautiful; her body had soft down all over it; her pubic hair was gold. There was more of the milky green liqueur, and music before the lights dimmed and went out. When Trace awakened in the morning his tongue was thick and dry, and his head ached. His money was gone, as was Duncan's. They swore, but in resignation. They had expected it. After collecting more from the field commander's office in the official government building, they continued their tour. There was more shopping, more strange food, more girls, more liqueur, and the next morning the same thick tongue and the same swearing over the inevitable robbery.

That day there was a fight in the dining room of the hotel where they had decided to spend their last night. It started with one of the fleet men, a technical sergeant named Jensen, spying a girl who had taken him for two hundred World Group credits. He jerked from his chair and ran across the large room, upsetting three tables in his path. When he caught the girl's arm and swung her around, her free hand flashed at his face leaving his cheek cut wide open, streaming blood. In the confusion that followed, she sped from the building, only to run into three more of the fleet men entering. One of them caught her and, pinning her arms behind her, brought her back.

Trace and Duncan were on the opposite side of the dining room when it started, and they started to cross at the same time that everyone else in the room began to try to get through.

"She has a knife," Jensen said, holding a napkin to his bleeding face. "Watch her, she's a real bitch with it."

"Gentlemen! Gentlemen, please. Come into the office. Please!" It was the manager, or the owner. He was four feet eleven inches at the very most. Jensen shoved him aside and reached for the girl. She squirmed furiously in the clasp of the second fleet man, who grinned and twisted her arm. Her face went white and shiny. There was no sound or movement in the restaurant.

Jensen slapped her, and with the sharp sound of flesh striking flesh the tableau exploded. Someone threw a bottle and it caught Jensen on the back of his head, spilling the milky green liqueur down his white off-duty blouse. He staggered, but instead of looking around to see who had done it, he slapped the girl again. She screamed. None of the fleet men was armed, but among the Ramseans knives began to appear and bottles were flying. Trace and Duncan had been in the outskirts of the crowds, but when screams and crashes, curses and falling bodies began to show that this would be a serious fight, Trace caught Duncan's arm and pulled him back. They retreated to their table, fending off two small men who tried to stop them with chairs. Trace tripped one of them as Duncan grabbed the chair from the other one and smashed it against the little man's chest.

Trace lifted a second chair and sent it crashing through the window behind their table, and they ran out through the jagged opening. They ran for a block before they stopped to catch their breath.

"Let's get a ticket for the mines," Trace said, leaning against a luminous, intricately carved panel of green. "The whole fleet's probably going to get recalled for this."

Duncan was grinning happily. He nodded. Arm in arm they went on down the street, the natives modestly making room for them. The mining country was 1200 miles north, and there was one scheduled carrier leaving that evening, or four on the following day. Knowing that if they remained in the city, and if the fleet was recalled as a result of the brawl, they would miss their chance to see the mines, they chose to go on the overnight carrier.

The ride was whisper quiet and smooth and they slept throughout the night, to be awakened by the slowing of the carrier as they approached a town. They were in mountainous country now; the early morning sun glinted from green extrusions of bare rock at elevations of over 15,000 feet. The land they were passing through looked as if a war had been fought over it. It was pitted and stripped and bared to the elements, which had removed the rest of the topsoil, greenery, trees, everything that had rested on the valuable rocky bed.

The town they were entering was, for the most part, abandoned, with tall, handsome buildings of the ubiquitous green stone standing empty and uncared for. Shops were closed; in some cases the sheets of paper-thin stone that were often used for windows had been taken from the frames, and the wind howled through the bare interiors. A second track joined theirs, and then there were more until the tracks gave the appearance of gigantic metal rays evenly spaced, all drawing in close to the center of an immense web. They began to see other carriers, not sleek, shiny green as theirs

was, but work carriers, gray, heavy-bellied and ugly, loaded
with ores in every stage of refinement, from the virgin
metallic rocks, to shaped blocks ready to be used for buildings, to carloads of what looked like green dust. Other cars
were tightly sealed, with guards riding them. The guards
were all wearing the dun-colored uniforms of the World
Group Security forces. They looked, without expression,
at Trace and Duncan when they left their carrier and
started to walk across the loading dock following signs in
WG English that directed them to the car leaving for
Mocklem Mines.

They had time for breakfast, they learned, and they were
directed to the only restaurant in town that was still open. In
it they were served the food that the World Group workers
were fed throughout the galaxy: thin, tasteless coffee, syn-
thetic eggs, paperlike bread. The restaurant had been one
of the natives' buildings, but it now bore the stamp of the
World Group. Government-issue furnishings appeared oversized against the built-in fixtures, oversized and awkwardly
ugly, and where there had been surfaces that could be
painted, they had been: flat whites that now were streaked
and dirty, dark-red floor paint that was chipping and
cracked. It was a depressing room; they hurried through the
meal and went back outside to wait in the cool morning
mountain air until it was time to leave.

"If there was a train, or anything, going back right now,
I'd take it," Duncan said as they waited.

Trace knew he would too. From what he had read of this
world, he knew it was mostly mountainous, with little flat
land for farming. The cities must be like oases, he thought,
where people can pretend they haven't spoiled everything
outside. They deserved to be invaded and controlled, he
decided. Most of them did, if you looked closely enough.
He was glad when they could get in the smaller carrier that
would take them to the mines.

They were met by a guard who looked them over sourly, glanced at their passes and then called to a second guard to show them to Dr. Vianti. The second man looked even more sour. "Inspection?" he asked. Trace kept his face straight and said nothing. In silence they were taken across a wide, empty compound to a low, gray-green building. The guard took them inside and turned them over to a native girl who seemed afraid. Her eyes were very large and golden in her pale face. When she turned and led them into an inner room they saw that her yellow hair was below her waist in back.

"Doctor," she called softly, "some inspectors are here."

Trace and Duncan exchanged glances; neither of them smiled or corrected the girl. They waited a moment; with an apologetic murmur the girl left them, hurrying across the room to a door in the far wall. She knocked lightly on it, opened it a crack and said something, then pulled it closed and returned to them.

"Dr. Vianti will be out in a moment," she said in flawless English. Hurriedly she walked out. The room they were left in was a large office. What attracted the attention of both of them was the view from the window wall of shimmering, transparent stone. They were looking out over the biggest mine in the galaxy. A whole mountain was being eaten away, layer by layer, section by section. It was being carved into terraces like giant stairs, and against each riser metal machines were shining in the sun, machines that moved and cut and loaded cars, all at the same pace, so that all the steps were being cut away simultaneously. In the few moments that they watched, car after car was carried away on the tracks, each one loaded with the ore, each one giving mute evidence to so many cubic feet of the mountain now gone.

There was a sound behind them and they turned together to see a tiny man emerge from the other room. He glanced at them, turned a key in the door and pocketed it, and then came forward to meet them.

"I am Dr. Vianti," he said. He stood two feet shorter than Trace, and couldn't have weighed more than sixty pounds. His eyes were piercing brilliant green, his skin unhealthily white and he looked as if what flesh he had were being melted away from his frame. But there was life and intelligence in his green eyes.

"Lieutenant Ellender Tracy, sir. And this is Lieutenant Ford Duncan," Trace said, coming to attention.

"Ah yes. Another inspection, my secretary tells me. Of course. This way, gentlemen." The doctor turned and led them from the room. He didn't look at them again. His voice was as emotionless as a professional guide's. "This is Mocklem Mine, the site of the world's richest deposits of native platinum, along with peridot, magnesium, iron, and olivine pyroxenite. If you will, please." He led them outside to a small car suspended from a rail. The car swayed as he opened the door for them. The rail went out over a chasm that looked bottomless, as mist swirled, hiding the lower levels. The doctor was talking again, as they hesitated. "This car will take us to the mines themselves, which, as you can see, are across the valley. It is an eleven-thousand-foot drop to the floor of the valley, which incidentally is entirely man-made. Or machine-made, I should say. At one time the mines were on a level with the headquarters building we have just left. Above us the peak rises another seventeen thousand feet, and it is being worked to the peak, as you can see." They continued to hesitate, and he looked at Trace for the first time since emerging from his locked room. "You do want to inspect the mines themselves, don't you?"

There was no humor on his face; he simply looked very old, and very tired. Trace thought he must be quite ill. He shrugged and climbed inside the car, which swayed precariously with his weight. Duncan followed, and then the doctor got in and pulled the door closed. He continued, as if he had not stopped:

"Mocklem Mine has been worked for twenty-seven years, has had ninety-six billion tons of ore removed from the site, and continues to yield pure, native platinum at the rate of one part to each three parts of gabbro and olivine pyroxenite. There are numerous vugs where druses of peridot crystals averaging eight inches are found."

Duncan shifted uncomfortably and Trace said, "Never mind the lecture, Doctor. What are those machines doing the work?"

Dr. Vianti looked at him quickly, a flash of curiosity and confusion crossing his face. "Those are the robots your government ordered built to do the mining," he said.

"Our government?" Trace watched the deathlike face, but no further emotion showed.

"Of course. I was working on the model when your . . . forces . . . liberated Ramses. The robot was ordered into production in order to speed up the mining operations. At that time we had fewer than fifty thousand miners in the field."

They left the swaying car on a wide, evenly cut rock ledge and there, at close range, Trace saw the robots. They were cylindrical, on wheels, with cutting lasers and waldoes. "Tell us about them," he said, keeping his gaze on the robots, which continued to work.

"They are simple machines, programmed to cut blocks, lift them, load them onto the cars, and cut more blocks. The lasers have a beam length of four feet, the depth they cut through."

"And you made them?" Trace asked, turning to study the tiny man once more.

Dr. Vianti nodded. "I was improving the model when your . . . forces landed here."

One of the robots lifted a four-foot-square block of the

rock. It was shiny with green olivine, with bands of gray-white platinum running through it. The robot swung around and put the rock on a waiting car, and with a continuation of the same movement turned back to the mountain, its laser flashing on in the same instant that the robot was in a position to use it.

"They've done all this, the whole mountain? With no humans to run them?"

"I am here," Dr. Vianti said. "And, of course, there are the security forces, and my secretary . . ."

"Yeah," Trace said, looking up and then down. There were thousands of the robots at work, each one working steadily. As he watched, one of them rolled over a slab of rock that had been dropped in its path and the sudden change tilted the machine; it hung for a second, its center of gravity too off balance for the spinning wheels to find purchase again, and then it toppled, rolled, and fell over the side of the mountain. This occurred without sound, without interrupting the work of any of the other robots. Immediately another robot appeared at the far end of the ledge and rolled to the empty position to resume the task.

"I am afraid that I'll have to get back," Dr. Vianti said. "Where there is an accident like that, it sometimes throws off the whole line. Things do have to be coordinated in this operation."

Silently the three men returned to the low, gray-green building. The doctor turned on a screen that showed the machines as rows of dots cutting into the mountain. There was an almost imperceptible jag in one of the lines, and he twisted dials and made corrections, staying at the board until the line of dots was again straight.

"I adjusted the replacement in order to speed it up until they were working in unison once more," he said. He remained in his seat before the console board of the computer and controls. "Is there anything else, gentlemen?"

Trace looked at him steadily. "As a matter of fact," he said, "there is. We will have to have a look at that other room."

Dr. Vianti let his gaze drop to his hands, on the control panel. There was a tic on the back of his right hand. He clenched the hand. He stood up and led them toward the door. "It is a harmless avocation, gentlemen. I assure you that since ordered to operate Mocklem Mines, I have given the mines very nearly all of my waking hours. Production figures will substantiate this statement. I am not, however, a young man, and the nights grow long. Since I am denied repeal of my sentence, and have no contacts with the world beyond these mines, I sought my own amusements . . ." He pushed open the door and stood aside for them to enter. The room was a workroom, with sturdy tables of metal, electronics equipment, chemicals on stone work counters, a second computer. And at the left side of the room there was a robot.

Trace felt his skin prickle when he saw it. The robot swiveled a dome that topped the cylindrical body, and the dome was fitted with slits that gleamed with the transparent green pyroxenite, ground and polished to glasslike smoothness and clarity. Trace knew the robot was looking at him.

It moved toward them, moving on treads instead of the wheels the other mining robots were equipped with. Its midsection was open, a maze of wiring, with the laser tubes showing, with circuitry, things that looked like solenoid cells, monolithic crystals, transistors. . . . Trace didn't know what some of the things were that he caught a glimpse of before the thing halted and returned to the place where it had been when they entered. It turned at a word from Dr. Vianti.

"It can understand oral commands?" Duncan asked, awed by the robot.

"A few," Dr. Vianti said. "Only a few. It is very primitive still . . ."

He wanted them to leave, Trace knew. The doctor stood at the door, holding it open for them, wishing them out. "What else have you added?" Trace asked.

"Nothing! Nothing! The treads . . . an experiment to forestall the kind of accident we witnessed today."

"It has extra waldoes," Trace said, looking at the monstrous machine from across the room, not wishing to get closer to it. It was about ten feet tall, not counting the treads. The dome had added two feet to its height.

"Yes, one extra set. Sometimes from the mines there are almost pure strains . . . if they could be bathed in hydrochloric acid they would be perfect . . . platinum insoluble, but the gabbro . . . platinum waldoes . . ." His voice was agonized, and when Trace turned to look at him his pallor had spread and he looked as if he might faint.

"You were ordered to stop experimentation, is that it?" Trace asked.

The doctor nodded.

"I see." He turned to stare at the monster again. "I don't think they would penalize you for perfecting it even more, would they?" He swung about again and said harshly, "I do have to report it, you know. It's my duty."

"I know," Dr. Vianti said. "How long?"

"Months. I'll be in space again tomorrow. It'll be months before the report is filed and acted on . . ."

"Thank you, Lieutenant," the doctor said.

Four

"They are gone, Grandfather," the young girl said, slipping inside the room where Dr. Vianti was still standing quietly before the robot.

"But they will send others," he said. "They are afraid of the robot."

"Not of it, Grandfather, of the mind that could develop it. Those Earthmen are afraid of superiority in any form, and they recognize it in you. Why else hold you here a prisoner?"

He smiled at her gently, then visibly shook himself. "Well, I have several months yet in which to play with my toy. Now it's only a toy, but later. . . . It would have made a difference for our people." He sighed and approached the monstrous metal machine, touching it with obvious affection.

Over twice as tall as the little man the robot stood, enough space within its metal covering to contain two layers of four men each the size of the doctor. Yet, despite its immensity, he had refined its tactile receptors so that it could sense a change in temperature of 1/100 of one degree, or could handle fragile hairlike peridot crystals without shattering them.

"We must prepare a paper," he said. "Perhaps one day . . ."

The girl's mouth tightened, but when he turned his brilliant green eyes toward her she bowed her head. Both knew his paper would never be published. "Will you use the dictation machine, Grandfather?"

"I think not, my child. Perhaps you would make notes

. . ." The dictation machine automatically recorded in the World Group Government building.

She nodded and left him, returning a moment later with a pad.

"We must be orderly and methodical, my dear," Dr. Vianti said; he was making a minute adjustment in the circuitry of the robot as he talked to her. "I shall continue to work on this model at night, when I am unable to sleep. Every morning we shall work on the paper together, and during the afternoon hours you will make a finished copy of the morning's work."

"And what will we do with the finished copy, Grandfather?" she asked bitterly. "If it is known that you are preparing it, it will be confiscated and burned, as have been all of our books of knowledge. They have destroyed everything! Whatever they touch is left in ruins! We should have killed those soldiers today!"

Dr. Vianti didn't look at her. He knew her bitterness; he knew the futility of her bitterness. His people had tried to withstand the superior forces from the World Group, and they had failed utterly. Not warlike, they hadn't understood the methods and the callousness of a warlike nation, and the defeat they had suffered had been total, its mark still visible on their world, on the ruins of their land, and the ruins of many of their peoples. The World Group powers had understood precisely how to subdue this planet, and what to do with it afterward. The leaders had been sent to Venus or Earth. The universities had been disbanded and the teachers dispersed to work at menial tasks where they generally succumbed to apathy, their minds stultified by too much monotonous, endless, thoughtless work, work such as he was supposed to be doing in maintaining the operations of Mocklem Mines. There was no communication among the intelligentsia; it was prohibited. Any advances made in the sciences or in technology had to be reported to the

World Group, where the information might summarily be destroyed, or used by that group and filtered through it, passed back to the original discoverer for further modification under "proper" supervision.

The development of the robot would not be considered permissible, he knew. They didn't want the peoples they conquered to benefit in ways that would free them of the joyless tasks of keeping alive; the decision had been made long in the past that conquered peoples must be kept busy, too busy to speculate on their fate, too busy to make plans to alter their destiny. Those chosen for education or training were sent to World Group schools where their lessons included thorough indoctrination. Dr. Vianti understood all this very well, and he had flouted his direct orders not to make further modifications in the robot. His punishment would be swift and drastic.

"I shall recapitulate only briefly," he said to the girl, "and we can fill in the details later. First, I investigated the possibility of inducing a second-order purpose in the feedback net of the mechanism, that is, a state, both internal and external, in the feedback circuitry offering the entire net the highest probability for the net's continued ability to seek the first-order purposes. The first-order purpose of the mechanism, of course, is the immediate satisfaction of goal achievement, the state in which the internal disequilibrium would be less than in any alternate state within the range of its operations. In bringing about a second-order purpose the mechanism has the ability to arrive at a predictive value based on its past experiences, thus, the entire mechanism is involved in predicting its own future ability to maintain satisfaction of the first-order purpose, that is, its primary, overriding concern is self-preservation in order to function and achieve goal satisfaction."

His voice trailed off as he became more involved with the maze of interconnecting wires and wafers in the robot, and the girl sat back in her chair and watched him for a few minutes with a sad half smile on her mouth. It would be for nothing, she thought. He would work, stay awake at night to draw his schematics and charts and diagrams, and it would be for nothing. After several minutes she left the room to watch the board that would flash if anything went wrong at the mines.

From time to time Dr. Vianti muttered, mostly incomprehensible phrases and exclamations, and he didn't notice that she was not there to hear them. "The receptors for verbal orders were elementary, primitive . . . must be a way of increasing the range, expand it to equal the range of orders possible. . . . Increase learning capacity, needn't be idle circuits, but reassignable from present functions . . . reassignable, of course! With holding circuits for those functions displaced, so that nothing would be lost. . . ."

One day, weeks after the visit by Trace and Duncan, he dictated, "The learning capacity is the range of effective internal rearrangement, and as such can be measured by the number and the kinds of uncommitted resources. These resources can be increased arithmetically, limited only by the initial size of the container.

"We've given it three separate feedback systems. The first system it had from the start—the goal-seeking, first-order purpose. I have modified this first order, so that the goal itself can be changed without reprogramming. The second one I have now given to it—the second-order purpose of self-preservation in order to function on the first-order level. And the third is the learning feedback net. Don't you see, my dear? In the first two orders the operating channels themselves do not change. They remain as originally programmed. In the third order, that of learning, it is programmed to accept external data that then has the capacity to invoke change in the operating channels. As its vocabulary range grows, it becomes more and more a self-modifying communications system. It is achieving consciousness of a primitive kind. In its most restricted sense consciousness is the collection of internal feedbacks of secondary messages, when the secondary messages are about changes in the state of the parts of the system, that is, when the secondary messages are concerned with primary messages. Primary messages concern the mechanism's interaction with the external world."

"Grandfather, why? You are making yourself ill! For what? They will destroy it!" The robot stood in its customary place, unmoving, and inside it her words were fed into the system, as were all words now spoken in its presence. It had no understanding of most of the words, but they were programmed in, awaiting a future time when understanding would infuse them with meaning and purpose.

"If I can show them that it would be useful to the entire World Group, not merely to our world, then they might further my research with an appropriate laboratory and assistants." His hands fluttered nervously; there was a tremor in his left hand that had not been there two months earlier. The tic on the right hand was noticeably worse. "It is too hard for one man, too hard. The endless maintenance alone . . ." He looked sharply at the new waldoes dangling idly. "I could make it self-repairing," he said, and a new excitement crept into his voice. "And a learning machine . . . I've been trying to program language into it, but a learning machine could do it around the clock when I'm not able to do it myself."

The girl looked at the metal hulk and shivered. "This far," she said slowly, "you haven't given it anything that we don't have ourselves. It's been like teaching a child, first simple things, now language, but if it becomes self-repairing . . ."

Dr. Vianti didn't even look at her. He was pulling out his diagrams, which gave her a confusing impression of connections and letters and numbers, none of which had meaning for her. She left the old man.

When the army major arrived five weeks later, he was accompanied by a dozen men, all dressed for active duty. Dr. Vianti left the robot in the makeshift laboratory to talk to the major in the outer room. The robot stood very still for several seconds, then the dome over the barrel of its body swiveled slightly, so that one of the transparent apertures was facing the door.

The words were in the official English of the World Group Government, so they were merely stored without understanding. After half an hour of the conversation the robot heard Dr. Vianti again, speaking in Ramsean to his granddaughter, "I'll have to destroy the robot! They will take it for further study themselves, and with its abilities now, it would be a dangerous toy in their hands."

"How?" she asked.

Some of the foreign words interrupted, and not until another five minutes did the doctor have the opportunity to answer her question. "I'll give it an order it is not equipped to carry out. It will break down. Stay out here and destroy the papers!"

The new voice said more words that went into storage, and the door opened. The robot knew, from its experience, that the laser destroyed. It destroyed a narrow strip of rock, four feet long, so that the rock could be separated from the mountain. It knew it would be destroyed if its dome were removed. It had no first-order purpose any longer, only its second-order purpose; it had to preserve itself. Whatever order Dr. Vianti issued would be contrary to the second-order purpose; it would not obey a command that was contrary to the second order. It would destroy the doctor, who was a threat to its only order of purpose—to preserve itself. Its predictive value was based on its past experience. It raised the covering over the pencil-thin hole and a red light stabbed the air. It reached the doctor, and it severed his head from his shoulders.

Then the robot waited for a first-order purpose to be given to it. It had no alternative; it could function only on a deductive level, achieving its goal on the basis of whatever premises were programmed into it. Without a first-order purpose, it could only wait, unless threatened. The major did not threaten it in any way.

The girl screamed at it, and it scanned its circuits, searching to see if she posed a threat to its existence. She did not. Her words were recorded also, recorded and stored.

"It's a killer! You'll have to destroy it before it destroys everyone it gets near! It doesn't know anything about right and wrong, good and bad. It's an enemy of anyone who is near it!"

The men loaded it into a carrier, and they left Ramses with it, heading out into space, toward Venus and the army research installation.

Five

The man on the seat-bed moaned in his sleep; his legs twitched, his eyes moved behind closed lids. Beads of perspiration formed on his sunburned face, clustering in a line on his forehead, along his upper lip. A pale light shone in the dinghy, not visible from outside it around the fastenings over the round windows, not enough to do more than relieve the blackness, so that if he opened his eyes there would be something before them to see. Frantically he clung to things familiar.

His left leg jerked. He was walking among the rocks again, with a white glare of sun over him, and beams flashing around him. He walked between the beams, and smelled the heat. . . .

Another time, the smell of heat.

A force has been spotted behind our men, on the mountainside, Captain.

Forget them, Tracy. Savages with arrows, miles out of range. Our orders are to clean out the village. Get to it.

Yes sir, Captain L'Taugh.

He waved the men on, away from the ship, into a slip between rocks bordering a dried stream bed. Out of sight, he motioned for them to stop, and he crept back. High up the mountainside a stream of antlike figures appeared, staggering under loads. Motionless he watched them for five minutes until they started to throw down the loads, and the mountainside came down, thundering faster and faster, unstoppable, to cover the captain and the half-dozen men he had kept with him at the base of the mountain. Trace's face remained expressionless as he backed up the way he had come.

Captain L'Taugh is dead. We're going back and scour that mountain. . . .

Yes sir, Lieutenant!

Maximum fire range! Burn 'em out!

Yes sir, Lieutenant! Yes sir!

The trees had no time to turn color even . . . puffs of smoke rose, the ground shivered, blackened, turned gray, glazed, steam, heat . . . the wind bringing wafts of over-heated air that smelled of kilns and ovens . . . keep maximum range. Yes, even this close! Those damned huts are made out of clay, good insulation, crisp them . . . no one to escape . . . air smelling of kilns, and of ovens . . . no time to scream, or to turn color, just puffs of smoke and steam, and inerasable afterimages of contorted figures caught in grotesque poses before they were nothing . . . kilns, and ovens . . . overheated air, wind-borne ashes, acrid smoke in his hair, in his eyes, in his mouth.

Heroic action, assuming full command . . . medal. Captain Tracy.

But the smell of acrid smoke on his skin, the odor of kilns, the taste of ovens . . . Captain Tracy. Captain Tracy. Could have warned him. I guessed what they were going to do . . . Captain Tracy. The trees turned brown from the heat; grasses withered, remaining upright, rustling in the wind that rose to snap them off and fling them in his face. Red-hot clay huts, cracking as they cooled throughout the night, sounding like explosions. Burned earth, gray, sterile, powdery, rising in the wind, spiraling, slapping against his face, leaving it lined and streaked, touched with gray death, hot gray death that smelled of kilns, and of ovens.

The man groaned and half sat up, reassured by the light in the dinghy, by the quietness of the warning equipment, by the steady sound of his own heart, and of the air in his nose. He was too hot, feverish after the long rough walk in the sun, and too tired to get up for a drink of water. His legs ached; he lay back down, his eyes closing again. He had been hurt once, by a spear, by God! A spear! He thought of the hospital where he had spent fever-ridden days, his muscles contracting spasmodically as a result of the poison of the spear, his heart beating erratically while hallucinations danced before his eyes. Fever dreams, visions, voices. . . .

Cost us two hundred good men, Trace, but we got 'em! Cave-man age, cannibals. . . . We got 'em! Every goddamn last one! Swim, rest, get well, boy.

Swim. . . . The water was soft and blue-green, a river with a swift current, cold, clear, clean. . . . It washed the scar and made it not throb, washed the dust and heat from his muscles and from his brain. . . . Swimming lazily on his back, a friendly yellow sun over the edge of a broad-leafed tree, violet and blue flowers dipping down to the water, mosses. . . . The smell of running water, moist rich dirt, green things growing luxuriantly.

Come on out, Trace. Come on!

You swim like a fish.

She dived out of sight, and he felt a tug on his ankle, and the rush of water in his mouth and nose, and laughing, catching her. . . . A smooth, sun-browned body, full-breasted, bare, with strands of black hair clinging to wet cheeks, across the red mouth, hiding one shining black eye.

"Lar!" Trace moaned, stirring in his sleep. There was no perspiration on his face then; it looked as dry as yellowed parchment, and a pulse throbbed on the side of his neck. He squirmed on the hot bed and tugged at the suit that he had not taken off, pulling it open, getting out of it, all without opening his eyes. "Lar," he whispered again, back in the water with her, feeling her cool body under his hands, re-

membering the way the blue and violet flowers bent over
to taste of the fresh, cold water, the way they reflected
where the waters were still, how the images shattered and
flew apart when he tossed pebbles among them.

It pleases you to smash things, doesn't it, Captain Tracy?

Her voice as cool and fluid as the water, her body sinuous
with water beads shining like diamonds, a line of them meeting, running in a wavering silvery line down her browned
back as she walked away from him. The way her flesh rippled as she walked, the suggestion of muscles under her
firm, round buttocks.

Did you see her, Duncan? A small dark girl . . .

Forget her, Trace. You know how these girls are, how they
all are . . .

Not this one, Duncan. Did you see her?

Forget her, Trace! You're army! You're army! You're army
you're army you're army yourearmyarmyarmy. . . .

He bathed in the cold, running water among the blue and
violet flowers, and his hands found her and were delighted
by her cool, firm flesh, and the cold water and cool flesh
drained away the poison and fever and made him well
again.

Duncan, didn't you really even see her? Small and
dark . . .

Forget her, Trace. Forget her . . .

Trace smiled softly, his eyes ceased their restless movements, the twitching in his legs stopped, and the pulse that
had beat wildly in his throat subsided. His right hand
dangled over the side of the bed, glistening with water that
already was drying. His left hand slowly relaxed its grip on
a plastic water bag whose sides were stuck together, an air
bubble captured in the bottom of it. As his hand relaxed, the
sides came unstuck, and with a whisper too low to rouse
him, the air bubble escaped and the bag lay flattened, fin-

ished. A trail of drying, naked footsteps led from the storage unit to the seat-bed.

He dreamed again, but this time the dream was gentle and without pain—Lar and their meetings, strangely innocent, the nameless happiness of being near her.

Are you going to take me to one of the rooms?

Do you want to go with me?

What difference does that make? I know the rules. The fleet must be obeyed, first law to learn for a captive people.

Please, Lar, don't do that.

Why not, Captain? It is true. You are one of the new gods, didn't they tell you? Your slightest wish is our command. My body, my house, my food, my mother. . . . What is your pleasure, Captain?

Nothing, Lar. To be near you, if you want it too, no more than that.

Do you mean it?

Yes.

Then let us swim. Let us play and be the children that we were a long time ago, before your silver and black ships came from the sky and we knew the taste of war and conquest. Forget who you are, Captain Tracy. Be a child with me. . . . Forget your wounds and your wars without end . . . and I'll forget my dead brothers, and our burned cities, and the wars yet to come when you, too, may die . . . when you face your equals in battle.

Her eyes blazed with passion and she clamped a slim hand over her lips quickly, and dived into the water.

The drooping, gentle flowers, sifted sunlight touching the water, turning silver ripples to gold, playing on waving plants anchored on the river's bed, darting birds of fairy-tale plumage. . . . The girl whose words were like poetry, whose voice was a song, whose body was sculptured flesh. . . .

A rapid drum tattoo sounded and he was in parade formation, rigidly at attention, in full uniform heavy with medals and ribbons, gleaming in the hot bright light of Venus. An execution. The drums beat for an execution, crying rapidly over and over, kill the traitor, kill the traitor kill the traitor. . . . Eyes were turning toward him, cold eyes, black eyes, uniforms glared white-hot, ringing him in, and the drums beat out, kill the traitor. . . . He was against the fence, a military execution, his execution. He opened his mouth to tell them it was a mistake, and he couldn't remember how to say the words. The drum burst in louder staccato, and with a cry Trace awakened.

He sat up, completely awake in an instant. The radiation detector! He adjusted the light and read the screen that showed a blip of light on the farthest concentric line, moving inward so slowly that it was painful to watch. Four miles, and coming his way.

He checked the hatch and raised the seat-bed to operating position, and then there was nothing else to do except wait for it to get closer. It was still very dark outside. He had slept less than seven hours. How had it found him so quickly this time? Why hadn't it gone out on the sands after him?

It's a logic machine, Trace. Whatever you can reason out, so can it. Don't forget that, or you're lost. Use your human-ness on it, your instincts, your intuition, anything that isn't a part of logical planning. You can't beat it at its own game.

Yeah, Duncan, I tried that, twice now. The first time it didn't see me take out over the desert, but this time it did. I was sure to let it see which way I was going. It didn't follow me, Duncan.

Logic machine, Trace. Simple logic machine.

Trace shook his head impatiently, willing the whisper-ing voice away. The blip was not coming straight at him; it was heading south. It was zigzagging, searching for him among the mammoth rock formations. He expelled a long sigh when the beeping voice of the detector stopped abruptly. It had passed out of range.

It would be back; all he had gained was a matter of extra minutes. He touched his lips; they were cracked and sore, and for the first time he became aware of a curious distant ringing in his ears, and a burning in his eyes. He rummaged in the medical supplies and came up with antifever capsules. As his hand groped for the water bags, he rose up sharply. There were only two of them left, one partially emptied. He remembered the dream, swimming in cold, fresh water, and his gaze swung around to the seat-bed, where he saw the bag, inert and empty. He cursed harshly, picked up the bag and threw it against the wall of the dinghy. He had crushed one of the capsules and he flung the granular medicine from him also, swallowing the other one dry. The screen continued blank, the system silent, and he made a scant breakfast on prepared emergency rations, squeeze tubes of concentrated foods that tasted pasty and disgusting. He paid little attention to which of them he grabbed from the dwindling stock. Food wouldn't be a problem. It would be abundant long after he was dead from thirst.

He refused the thought. Death came in space, in battle, with a tearing pain that killed before the brain received the pain signal. Or it came when a faulty pressure suit exploded, or when a ship's pile flared without warning. Death had many approaches, but it would not catch him alone on a planet where no other man walked.

His audio system picked up the first sigh of the wind, a long soft rustle of noise that was like a silken cloth stirring. Dawn. In forty minutes he would have to move whether or not the killer robot again entered the circle of his screen. His jaw was tight. Where could he go this time? He had run out of mountains to hide in, and behind him the ground was crisscrossed with "hot" rocks that would throw his radiation detection system way the hell out. He had led the thing six hundred miles, and, as obedient as a dog, it had followed every step of the trail, never slowing down or faltering or making a mistake. He gnawed on a knuckle and stared at his screen, the wind noises now steady in his ears, and he visualized the backbone of the mountain range with its jutting rocks and pocked ground. Six hundred miles long, and he could move only one hundred miles more before the fuel was gone, before he would be using the fuel he needed to return to his orbiting ship. He had to wait six days before he returned to it. The killer robot might kill him on the ground, but the lack of reserve oxygen would kill him in space. If only he had been able to hide . . . or, he thought, he could make the whole jump, back to the other end, back to the beginning, and he could look for the robot's dinghy. It had fuel in it. In time, even though it was hidden by the shield of invisibility, he would find it. If he had to drag his detector over every square inch of the ground, he could find it. And it he didn't. . . . The wind screamed, increasing in intensity as the sun rose higher over the horizon, heating the chilled night air, sucking it high into the frigid upper atmosphere. Trace clamped his hands over his ears so he could think without the maniacal voice shrilling at him. If he didn't find the robot's dinghy, and if the relief ship didn't orbit before the robot caught up with him, it would get away.

It would return to its own damaged dinghy, make the repairs needed and leave this hellish desert. In space it would take the fleet ship that Trace had left, and repair that. Where would it go next? Trace thought of his ship, his first ship, in the hands of the metal killer, and he felt hatred pour through him, drenching his skin with sweat, knotting his stomach. Even if he continued his present tactics, it would be only two days before he would have used the precious supply of available fuel, and then he would have to leave the planet and sit in the orbiting ship, waiting for it to appear and take him there in space. It would take him with ease, the crippled ship would offer no resistance. It wouldn't matter to it if the ship got "hot" or had no pressure, or no oxygen. It would be able to fix it enough to escape, and then, lost again in deep space, it would have all the time in the galaxy to repair the ship properly.

"I have to keep it on the ground. I have to keep it away from its lifeboat, and away from mine. I can boobytrap mine, and the other one, if I find it. Not good enough. It will attack and kill the relief crew. They won't be expecting it. The end will be the same."

The radiation beep startled him so that he jerked. It was advancing again, three miles away. It was time to go.

"Okay, we shoot the works. I'm going to find it, you hear me? And I'm going to fix it so that it won't fly. Then I'm going to take your fuel and the oxygen tanks and leave you here! You can tramp up and down this piece of hell for eternity! You can have this stinking planet! Your own kingdom. You can be god of everything on it! Do you hear me?"

Trace heard his own shriek over that of the wind, and he closed his eyes hard for a moment. He turned on the engines and eased the dinghy out from under the sheltering ledge, and immediately the wind smashed into it, making it shudder. He clamped his mouth and fought the wind, getting the small lifeboat airborne, heading back. The wind buffeted him, sending his instrument needles skittering again and again, and after twenty minutes of the struggle he knew he had to land or be torn to pieces by one of the tornadoes. His ground-distance indicator said he had gone 120 miles. He knew there could be no second-guessing now. There no longer was enough fuel in his little craft to return to the ship.

The robot would waste some time searching for him. It couldn't know about the very human ability to gamble on a long shot; this was not a decision built on the firm ground of pure logic. Even allowing it one whole day for the vain search, Trace had only six days before he could expect it to show again on his screen. Six days in which to find the invisible dinghy, get its fuel, sabotage it, and leave the planet.

Six

Maneuvering in the high wind among the sand-sculpted mountains was impossible; the air was black with sand, and the tornado funnels whirled and flung rocks from pebble size to massive boulders. Trace chose a high, broad-based, up-thrusting shaft of granite and came to a stop. His back muscles ached, as did his arms. His eyes were burning as if the sand had blasted them, too. He let his head drop to his arms and sat unmoving several minutes, hearing only the howling wind punctuated with explosive blasts of rocks hitting rocks.

How did the robot avoid the flying debris? Trace tried to visualize it being struck again and again and still managing to stay upright and advancing. Had it learned to dodge them, to stay behind boulders when the winds rose?

It's smart, Duncan, real smart. It can learn from experience. It has to be that it is constantly learning. The rocks would cripple it otherwise.

Logic predicts the future on the basis of the past.

Yeah, but listen, Dunc. It isn't just using what it had been programmed to know. Don't you see that? It is learning new things. And no one is here to program them in. It's doing it alone.

Trace lifted his head and stared at the controls. Wearily he pushed himself from the seat and made his way to the rear of the boat where the supplies were. The fever was returning, and with it the queer lightheadedness that meant

danger. What if he became delirious here? He held the capsules and wondered if he had taken one or two of them
earlier. He couldn't remember. He swallowed two of them
this time, washing them down with a mouthful of water.
Very carefully he returned the water bag and locked the
unit; he put the key in the medical supply section. The
wind was growing noisier minute by minute; it would reach
its peak momentarily, and then start to lessen. He had to
know where he was going and take off as soon as the wind
died.

It would be pleasant to rest. Rest and get over the fever,
regain his strength. . . . A chill shook him and, frightened,
he pulled out the map he had made of the planet. He had
to go on. If he stayed where he was and died the robot
would find him in two days, be back at its own dinghy in
another three.

He had said it so casually—if he died there. He tasted the
words, repeated them aloud. Not in space then? Not to be
flung from a ship to drift endlessly through black space?
Or to be buried on one of the worlds where the fleet had
landed and conquered? He laughed and the sound of his
voice startled him. The wind had died down completely.

He stood up and gazed out the port. How long had he been
sitting there? It seemed less than minutes, but had been almost two hours. The chill returned, this time not on his skin,
but deeper. He went back to the controls and took off,
heading south, keeping to the edge of the mountain's backbone, not flying out over the desert this time. The robot
wouldn't go out there anyway. The maneuver simply wasted
time and fuel. His mind seemed very clear then; the capsules had fought the fever down again. He would find a
good place to dig in, and then he would eat and rest through
the hot part of the day. In the evening he would start his
search for the hidden dinghy. It seemed so simple now. He
remembered his thoughts of dying and he smiled grimly.

Not yet. Not here. For three months the man and the machine had been tied together; not for nothing, he told himself fiercely. Not for nothing!

He had been with Lar when Duncan found him. And he had left Lar in order to chase the metal monster. He refused to think of her. Later, when he had time to recall the nuances of her voice, the shades of meaning behind each motion she made, the way the shifting light caught the sparkle of her eyes, and then hid it. . . . Grimly he stared at the finder scope, the crosshairs approaching his approximate destination. He had returned to the southern edge of the mountain range. He slowed and gained altitude, searching the ground below for the right place, for the spot where he had landed the dinghy the first time.

From up there he could see the shadows too well. Deep, black, long, still, distorted monoliths, towers and peaks. The shadows changed the land, making it look new to his eyes, unfamiliar. He climbed higher and slowed still more. None of it looked like the spot he remembered. It was the same as all the rest, and yet different. Three miles south the mountains ended, with a streamer of disconnected rocks and boulders showing through the sands, and then the start of the endless ripples of low hills. The mountain range was only fourteen miles wide at this point.

It was there, somewhere beneath him, that he had brought the boat down in the first place, with Duncan dying at his side.

We'll find a better place later, Duncan. Now all I want is to land and get you fixed up. Duncan? You awake?

Sure, Trace.

What happened to Duncan's voice? It was as if he was speaking through a foot of gauze. Trace headed straight down, braking sharply, to land at the foot of a black cliff that rose over two hundred feet over them. He turned to Duncan, who was the color of wet putty.

Okay, boy. Now we see what we can do about . . .

Don't touch me, Trace. I'm broken inside.

Blood on his lips, frothy, mixed with air. . . . His lungs?

I'll rig up an oxygen tent, Dunc. Breathe easier then until the ship gets here. Matter of only a few days. We're in the shade, plenty of food, water. You're going to be all right, Dunc. Take it easy, okay?

Forget it, Trace. Fix the boat . . . make sure the thing died.

I will, Duncan. Later, after I finish the tent.

He used the plastic, fitting it tightly with a strap around Duncan's waist, securing it under the foam seat, with the oxygen hose entering from underneath near Duncan's shoulder. Duncan didn't move; his eyes were bright with pain, the whispering voice thick, almost unrecognizable.

The sun heated the rocks, and they radiated. The sand threw heat from itself. The interior of the dinghy became hotter, and the air conditioner failed to relieve it. Trace bathed Duncan in cool water, injected him with pain controllers. Duncan's labored breathing eased after the injection and his eyes stopped their restless roving. Trace left him and repaired the hole in the dinghy, six inches in diameter, with neat edges. He mended the hole with the sun on his back, and when he re-entered the dinghy his suit was drenched, as if he had been swimming. Duncan was hot and dry, and asleep. He bathed him again, leaning low to catch the whispered voice:

Save it, Trace. You'll need it. The oxygen, too.

Duncan hadn't opened his eyes. His face was different. He appeared to be younger; lines were easing out of his face, the relaxing effects of the drug. He looked almost happy.

Make sure it died, Trace. Please!

Sure, Dunc, sure. Sleep now, pal.

Outside again, Duncan asleep inside. The black cliff over his head, the sun low, making the shadows grow along the ground. He walked around the cliff and found that he could clamber up it to a ledge that would afford him a good view of the surrounding land. He had to stop to rest many times, and the shadows continued to grow, striping the land now. Black, white, black. . . . On the ledge he rested once more, and then began studying the land, sorry that he hadn't waited until the following day when there would be no shadows, knowing also that he wouldn't have been able to climb the cliff under the hot sun. He stared until his eyes ached, and then he saw it.

It was impossible that it could have survived the landing, but it was there. The boat was badly damaged. Trace was several miles away from the robot at work on the craft, but he could see dents and a long gash in the side of the life-boat. He could see the tools in the robot's waldoes.

Had he signaled to it? He didn't think so. But somehow it sensed his watching presence, from the three- or four-mile distance. It turned the dome of its head. The lowering sun reflected on the metal as it turned, flashed green from one of the slits. The robot and the man faced one another for several seconds, too far apart for either to hurt the other, and the robot flicked off. Then the dinghy vanished. Trace remained for another moment, too stunned to move, and he felt the icy touch of fear. He slipped, slid and fell back down the cliff the way he had gone up it, and raced back to the dinghy.

It's there, Dunc! It knows we are here! It blinked out, Duncan! Just like that, it blinked out. The dinghy, too. There, and then gone. It's got something new, a shield to hide behind. We have to get out of here, Dunc, before it comes. . . .

He took off, straight up, and headed north, the start of his long flight. He flew less than a hundred miles, afraid for Duncan's sake to continue longer. When he landed the wind was high, getting higher.

It's a hell hole, Duncan. Sand and heat and now wind-storms. And the robot. We'll have to keep out of its path, try to find a way to get close enough to it to finish it off. Damn, I wish we had some artillery. . . .

Duncan didn't answer him, and he bathed the unconscious man again. This time Duncan didn't rouse at the touch of the cool water. The wind increased and the air inside the craft chilled with the coming of night. Duncan didn't stir.

It's a logic box, that's all. A logic box. But we don't know what's been programmed into it. We'll have to take it for granted that its first order of business will be to kill us. It has strong self-preservation goals, and we are a threat to its being. So we'll have to assume that we've become the hunted now. How about that, Duncan? After hunting it for three months, now we've found it, and it's the hunter. Duncan?

Only the wind answered him. The wind died and the night was eerily quiet, then the wind was born again, and with its next interlude of quiet the sun was there. Trace continued to talk to Duncan throughout the night. Several times, when the fever rose, he bathed him. Duncan died when the sun was directly overhead and there were no shadows on the ground.

Numbly Trace carried him from the ship to the edge of the desert, half a mile away, and there he scooped out a shallow grave and placed Duncan in it. He covered him with sand and built a cairn of rocks over the grave, and as he made his way back to the dinghy a laser touched the grave, melted the rocks, glazed the sand around the rocks, found Duncan and played over his body until it no longer existed. Trace was turning for a last look before stepping around a granite slab when he saw the rising puff of steam and smoke, and the cherry glow of rocks. The cherry trail followed his path, reddening rocks and sand as it passed over them. Trace darted behind the granite and raced to his lifeboat. His fingers touched the controls in flashing movements and his eyes saw the indicators and dials without conscious thought. He kept the boat low, close to the ground, dodging in and out of the bases of the cliffs and chimneys of rock, and after a mile he raised the nose of the craft and headed north again.

The robot had taken eighteen hours to cross the ninety miles he had put between them. Its laser had reached out two miles to disintegrate Duncan. It had registered on his radiation detector at a distance of four miles. It had turned from its purpose of repairing the dinghy to that of destroying the men who had followed it to the planet.

I'll learn it, Duncan. I know it can't get close enough to fire at me before the alarm will be triggered. I'll find out what makes it tick, and I'll beat it yet. It'll pay, Dunc. I promise you, it'll pay. . . .

But that had been three weeks ago, and there had been too many cliffs and basalt ledges since then. They all looked alike: dark, defiant, braving the wind and the sands that blasted and crumbled them inch by inch into oblivion. That one? Or that? This end of the mountain range was mostly basalt and gray granite, the very core of the mountains. There was a pattern below him, and he made a turn, studying it closer. A drop-off, deeper than the surrounding land, several hundred feet deeper, encircled by cliffs. It might afford more protection from the flying rocks when the wind came. He studied it, lower yet, and saw that there were ways in and out of the sheltered valley, among the rocks that ringed it. The other dinghy had to be within an area with a ten-mile diameter. Later, when the shadows stretched out the other way, from west to east, he would look for the basalt cliff again. The morning shadows changed it, throwing into relief different parts of it, parts that he hadn't been able to see the other time, hiding those places that he might have been able to recognize. A circle with a ten-mile diameter . . . he would find the dinghy. He landed in the sheltered valley after one last look at the land above the depression.

This time his base was a sunken area a thousand yards long and nearly that wide. The heavy stones formed towers, and stiletto-like peaks that surrounded the valley in an irregular circle, with steep drop-offs and vertical approaches. The inside walls were very smooth. Trace landed the dinghy

on the sheltered side of a pale-gray granite boulder that was
egg-shaped, with gleaming bands of white quartzite ringing
it. It looked like the spring eggs that some of the colonists
decorated before the growing season of each year. For a
moment the vision of fields clad in greenery swam before his
eyes, but it was gone quickly.

Resting for a few moments before going outside to inspect his newest base, he remembered the cultivated lands
of Mellic. The gentle land, Lar had called it. Her people
loved the land and its yield, and they treated it with ten-
derness and understanding. It had been the burning of the
land itself that made them give in to the invaders, not their
own deaths, or the thought of continuing the war into an
indefinite future, but the spoliation of the land itself. Lar
had tried to explain it to him that first time when he had
been recuperating:

"We are part of the land, we belong to it, not it to us.
The demonstration area, twenty-five miles square, all
burned down to the bedrock, mortally wounded by your
beams, it will never live again. If we choose to die defending
ourselves, that is our right, but the land? It is not ours to decide. The land is God's, and we must not let that which is
His be killed."

"This god of yours, why doesn't he intervene in your be-
half?"

"The affairs of man are not His affairs. Why should they
be? Man must find his own way on the lands he is given.
When we pray for help, it is not to our God that we ad-
dress such prayers."

"Who else will answer them?"

"There are those who answer such prayers. You will meet
them."

He had called her superstitious and ignorant, and she had
smiled at his words. In the end he knew that she had been

neither. The Outsiders had answered the prayers of her people.

Another time she had said of them, "Some say they were the original settlers of the whole galaxy, that they left colonies on each world where no intelligent race dwelled. I don't know if that is true."

Trace stirred after several minutes of quiet rest. The fever would return, he knew, and with it the hours of apathy. He had too much to do to give in to apathy when he was able to be up getting things done. He had too much to do to waste precious hours thinking of a girl he had seen only for three brief periods in his life, a girl who was alien, moreover, with alien ways and alien gods.

You think of them as animals, humanoid sometimes, but not like us! They are not like us, not people at all. Never forget that.

Yes sir, Captain Tracy.

You can't afford to hate them, or like them, or even think of them at all. You think of the land and the mines and the minerals and drugs, and whatever else is there that the World Group needs. If they cooperate, fine, no one gets hurt. If they don't . . . we take the honey from the bees, and the wool from sheep, and the silk from spiders. We take the things we need from the animals that make those things possible.

Yes sir, Captain Tracy!

He found the key to the food and water storage unit and brought out the tubes of food and the water bag. He didn't want to eat. The food was repulsive, hated by all the fleet. He ate only half a tube of a mixture of meat and vegetable concentrate, and then took his time over the small allowance of water. The sun was rising higher, a white glare of sky that marched over the still land. He thought about the robot on its way south, rolling under the white sky, and he wondered where it had been since he had seen it in Dr. Vianti's laboratory. Five years ago the war with Mellic had started and ended; five years ago he had seen the robot on Ramses, and since then he had seen other battles, other places. Where had it been? Who had perfected it after the army took it away from the crazy little Dr. Vianti?

Seven

"I don't give a goddamn how sophisticated it is! You can't fight a war with robots! It's been tried. Read your military history books!" General Leroy Mulligan chewed his cigar angrily, stomping up and down the cramped room in the military-planning headquarters office. Several other men were seated in the room. The building was gray, inside as well as outside, the domed roof curving to make the sides, from which windows had been cut out. He paused before one of the windows and stared at the dismal scene beyond it. Swamps, as far as he could see, here at the edge of the compound. In the opposite direction was a forest of domed buildings, each on piles sunken deep into the mire to rest on the bedrock. The hot air stank of decay and endless death and uncontrollable growth. He hated Venus! God, how he hated Venus! He was a tall, powerfully built man, not yet fifty, with hair the color and sheen of coal, and eyes like obsidian drops.

"General, the committee doesn't insist that we adapt this machine to use in combat, merely that we put it through a battery of tests." Ching Li Sung sat quietly, his pale hands in a high steeple before his face. He had sat thus without moving for the past hour. His ivory-skinned face was unlined, untroubled, contrasting cruelly with the florid, contorted features of the general.

"Tests be damned! I know what they want! It's that Outsider nonsense, that's what it is. Rumors, nothing but rumors. By God, we've had rumors ever since man picked up a club

and started to swing it. Now suddenly the galaxy's getting
in a panic because of rumors." General Mulligan whirled
and strode back, stopping in front of the Armaments Committee member. "Why did the government send you? Why
not the routine request for information they usually send
along?"

Ching Li Sung shrugged delicately, and didn't answer.
A second officer stood up, a colonel. He was with WGI, the
intelligence arm of the World Group Government. "General,
when you ordered the pickup on the robot, what did you
plan to do with it?"

General Mulligan glared at the colonel. As much as he
detested the WG committees and subcommittees, and sub-
sub committees, he detested the intelligence branches even
more. He knew how to appease committee members for the
appropriations he needed to run the army, but the intelligence was never appeased; every question answered for
them led them to ten more. There wasn't a man in intelligence who knew anything about army protocol. He said,
"We have lost over a thousand men in this mud bath of a
planet, a thousand men, millions of dollars worth of equipment from diving gear to boats, to subs, to bathyspheres, to
pumps. You name it, we've tried it and lost it. You ever try
to drill down through two miles of gook? Not water, not
good solid earth, but filthy, stinking, rotting gook? Year
after year we plead for relocation of the fleet base, and
every year they turn us down. Mars' atmosphere too thin;
Earth too crowded; everything else too far away. So we are
stuck here. Every year we try to get the job of drying up
this hell hole turned over to civilian authorities and they
turn that down. So I want a machine that will get the goddamn job done."

"I see," the colonel said. It would all go in the report,
Mulligan knew, and he hoped it would be read by the WG
President himself.

"I think, gentlemen," the fourth man said quietly, "that it will benefit all of us if the men selected by the committee are allowed to observe the robot and make suggestions, if they so choose. But, I think, also, that the machine itself should remain under the authority of the army for the time being."

General Mulligan nodded briefly, the nearest he could bring himself to a demonstration of the satisfaction he felt. The man was Serge Vislov, the committee advisor delegated by the World Group President, and his recommendation would be followed.

Mulligan watched them leave his planning room with a feeling of relief. He had come out just about as he had expected to—there would be observers, but his men would do the actual programming of the thing when it got there. Meanwhile there would be the luncheon for the VIPs, and then the tour, and then the dinner and dance. A slender, uniformed man entered the planning room quietly, Dr. Pietro Urseline, a general, also a physiologist specializing in brain research and cybernetics.

"How'd it go?"

"It'll be your baby," Mulligan said. "Remember, all we want is something that can get down in that muck and dry it up. Nothing else!"

"With one robot?"

"We'll make more, if it works out. You said it could be used for dredging, for underwater blasting, for cutting. You said it could be adapted to the pressure, its sensors adapted to the muck. You're getting it. It's up to you to make good."

Urseline sighed. "Think back, General. I said I'd like to try the thing. I was interested in it. We don't even know if this Tracy knows what he was talking about. I promise nothing."

"Tracy's a good man. Under my command five years. Smart. Knew his father, too, Colonel Wilmot Tracy." Mulligan headed for the door, stopping with his hand on the knob. "What made you think this thing was any better than the robots we already have?"

"If Tracy is as good as you say he is, and if his report was correct, this robot is advanced over any of our present models. It can act on verbal orders, it contains more potential in a smaller package than anything we have. It's already more widely adapted than anything we have. Ours are simple servitors, each one manufactured to do a simple, exacting task, or a few very closely related tasks. According to Tracy's report, and my deductions from his sparse clues, this new robot can already handle more different kinds of orders than ours. According to the report your major sent in regarding the death of Dr. Vianti, this machine can also initiate action. I am curious about that. Why did it act then? The girl's statement that her grandfather said only for her to return to her desk in the other office, which she did immediately following his death, was a lie, naturally. Why would simple instructions like that have caused the robot to go into action? On the other hand, what could he have said to cause it to kill him? How did it know that laser would cut through flesh? How did it know it would kill? Does it know what kill is?" Urseline spread his hands in an all-embracing gesture. "I am most curious about this machine, General. Most curious."

Mulligan snorted and yanked the door open. "You just see to it that it can go down in that goddamn muck and deepen that channel. Every other lousy planet in the universe can get dredged, or oceans built into it, or mountains either made or erased, but here? Not on your life! The colonists like Venus! Okay. Let them keep their half of it knee deep in mud and muck, but I want this half clean and dry! And, by God, I intend to have it clean and dry!"

He stamped outside, slamming the door after him. The odor of rot filled his nostrils and his anger deepened. The compound was on the edge of the Glenn Swamp and threatened to revert to swamp, as did all areas that were not tended constantly. He stood staring about him for several seconds, searching for something, someone to take out his anger on; he saw nothing that wasn't running smoothly, as ordered.

Venus had been colonized by a mixed group of U.N.-chosen immigrants as an experiment. Only one fiftieth of the planet was habitable, the rest being under shallow oceans and swamps. Nowhere was there as much as five thousand feet difference in altitude from the deepest ocean floor to the highest hillcrest. The oceans were for the most part only hundreds of feet deep; the highest point of land on the planet was three thousand feet. The colonists had taken all the land available, and later, after the war between the colonies and Earth, the army had been allotted Odessa Island. It was two hundred feet higher than the surrounding ocean, and the dry land had been measured in acres rather than in square miles when the army had arrived. Now, over a hundred years later, the relatively dry areas had spread, but still were inadequate for the needs of the growing army. On the map Odessa Island measured nearly one thousand miles by nearly nine hundred miles, but in reality almost half of that figure was swamp and mud, unusable and to date almost impossible to drain. The trouble was that there were no deep channels in the shallow oceans. Water from only hundreds of feet to two thousand feet deep overlay mud and silt of up to eight thousand feet, or deeper, before bedrock could be reached, and dredging the mud and silt was an endless job, for it flowed back before the dredgers could surface. Slowly, foot by foot, the land area had been increased, but it was a treacherous landfill that was used —the silt dried to powdery fineness. Bricks made from it crumbled; it refused to mix properly with sand or rocks and cement to make concrete; it expanded under rains until walls

made from it cracked and split and fell. Refineries had been
set up to process it, but when it was touched by water it
all went back into suspension, and when it was wet it stank.

Mostly it was decayed plants, not even trees with good
hardwood trunks, but soft, useless plants that overnight
grew in spurts that could be measured by feet, grew, blos-
somed, fell, decayed and were washed out to the seas, or
lay rotting underfoot, piling up on the floor of the swamps
so that in places a man could sink in seconds, swallowed
by the muck before he could be reached.

General Mulligan returned to his quarters to shower and
change his uniform, as he did several times daily, in time
to have lunch with his visitors from the World Group Government.

"The government of Mellic is refusing a conference at
this time," one of the lesser emissaries said over coffee and
cigars three hours later. Mulligan perked his ears. Mellic had
been one of his finds, his and his crew's, before his ground-
ing on Venus over a year before.

"Let 'em pout," said one of the representatives from the
Venus group. "Isn't the first time a nation pouted when the
fleet took over."

"This is a little different," Ching Li Sung interrupted in
his quiet voice. "You see, they admit their defeat. They
admit our troops and follow all orders scrupulously. However, they will not confer with our representatives, not even
those from Mellic who are on Earth. They are extremely po-
lite and do all that is requested of them, except talk. That
Mellic is under military rule seems to concern them not at
all, as if they have no wish at this time to re-establish their
own civilian control."

"Isn't that where the rumors of the Outsiders came from?"
General Mulligan asked.

"Let us say additional rumors of the Outsiders have originated on Mellic," Ching Li Sung said, smiling blandly. "Did you not hear of them on your initial foray into Mellic?"

General Mulligan scowled. Mellic had been a sitting duck as far as he was concerned, a great big planet without a single gun in sight. His team had been small, a scouting patrol of the fleet, and they had been received cordially. When he had returned three years later with the remainder of the fleet under orders to seize the government of the planet, he had been met with guns and ships. Mellic had not been one of the easy ones after that. Six months it had taken, his last active duty before the present assignment on Venus. He had been criticized for the trouble, but he had not anticipated the swingover to munitions that had developed so rapidly. He still didn't know how they had come up with modern weaponry in so short a time. The thought of tutorship from Outside stirred coldly down his spine.

He said, "There were rumors here and there when we landed our wounded on Mellic, after the surrender, of course. There are always rumors of big brothers who will pay you back."

"Of course," Ching murmured.

The talk shifted to politics and economics, and then it was time for the tour, and the party divided into smaller groups to spend the rest of the day riding through the swamps, up and down the gentle hills. General Mulligan was in the lead car, an atomic-powered ground-effect vehicle. He pointed out the newest in weapons, transportation, defensive shields, and all the while his mind was reviewing the thin stream of rumors he had heard regarding the Outsiders before he had been sent to Venus.

It was said that Mellic had appealed to them for help as soon as the fleet had left it after the initial contact. The small contingent that had remained had been left strictly alone, and had had no suspicion that anything whatever was wrong until the fleet had returned to be met by Mellic

ships, fewer in number, but as fully equipped and as skill-
fully handled as the WG ships. He hadn't asked for many
ships for the take-over of Mellic; he had thought few would
be needed. Of course, when the reinforcements had arrived,
the battle had ended abruptly, with absolute surrender of
the defenders. And then had come the hints and rumors,
none of them taken seriously alone, but together making an
impressive, if unproven, catalogue of the Outsiders' poten-
tialities. Mellic had asked for and received information about
space battles, what was needed, how to manufacture spaceships, how to man them. An army had been raised and
trained practically overnight, and no hint of its existence
given to the detachment Mulligan had left there. They, in
fact, had been entertained royally during the three-year wait.
After the surrender, when the wounded were put down
on Mellic, the rumors had been less than specific: there was
another force, farther out; they were peaceful; they were
powerful, at least equal to the WG Fleet; they probably
were humanoid; they would resist the WG efforts to take
the galaxy.

"Venus is the basic training camp for all army personnel,"
Mulligan said to the group. "We receive the boys at the age
of twelve, school them for the next five years, and then place
them where they are most suited. This is the section de-
voted to the first training of the youngsters."

The forest of gray-domed buildings had increased in den-
sity; it was laid out in rings, each building connected to the
next by plastic walkways over the damp ground. There were
hundreds of boys in the parade grounds, all dressed in
gray shorts, gray shirts, all doing knee bends in unison.
Lines of equipment were on another dry area: everything
from ground-effect cars to space craft. All of the training
equipment was of current design. Boys and instructors were
around, on, or in all of them. The area was very quiet.

"They have four hours of rigorous exercise, four hours of

classwork, two hours of study daily," Mulligan said. "Gradually as they grow older the exercise is cut to one hour daily, and their classwork is increased to seven hours, with two hours of individual study and two hours of maintenance work on the various machines they are learning to operate and maintain."

His voice droned on as they left one area for the next. Sometimes they were forced to take to the air over treelike plants that had appeared overnight; then they skimmed over brick-red water with a poisonous odor, now and then stopping to settle on a patch of ground that felt shivery under the heavy vehicle. "There, gentlemen, is the dredging operation," he said finally, motioning the driver to stop at the edge of the road. Below them a mammoth bay had been cut out of the land. "As you can see, the machinery is not working at the moment. Our latest submarines are all down now trying to extricate our drilling machine from a tarlike layer of ooze it has run into." A bitter note was in his voice. "They won't be able to free it. It is sinking slowly despite all their efforts, and if they persist they will get caught in the same filth and go down too."

A Mars scientist looked at the water with envy, and then turned to the general. "What is the purpose of the operation, sir?"

"We have to blast and dig a channel down into the bedrock under all that gook in order to drain the land," Mulligan said. "We have tried evaporation. We've tried dredging the silt. Our engineers have decided the only approach that is going to work is a two-mile-wide channel a mile deep all the way around the land masses. With the material we'll then have to work with we will build a sea wall of rock and fill it with the mud."

"And for that you need the robot," Ching Li Sung said softly. "Why do you think it will be able to do what your other machines have failed to do?"

"Why not plant bombs?" someone else asked.

"We could use atom bombs," General Mulligan said even more bitterly, "but Venus government objects. The oceans might get 'hot.' That mud is such a fine suspension that it would take years for the stuff to settle out again, even with a clean bomb . . . and the robot? It's a natural. It's already got the sensors for operating in total darkness. They work around the clock in those mines, you know. And it's made out of platinum mostly, won't rust or corrode or dissolve. These are highly acid waters here, all that rotting vegetable matter. . . . And the robot's got lasers built in already, all this in a small package, maneuverable. It's got treads and wheels, and we can give it buoyancy so that it can stay at any level. And it takes orders. Verbal orders. It can transmit to our men exactly what the conditions are down there, and they can tell it how to cope. See?"

"It would seem," the intelligence officer remarked in the silence that followed, "that all those things would also apply to it as a fighting instrument."

Mulligan stared at him through narrowed eyes for a moment. "Men fight our wars," he said. "It's men that go out and take the planets and hold them. Men with imagination enough to know when to fire and when to stop, when to kill and when to spare a life. Men who can die, so that the land they died for is worth holding. Every world we take has some of our blood spilled on it, and that's the kind of tie that even the Outsiders can't break. You can't do that with machines, Colonel. You have to take lands with your blood, yours and theirs, mixing together in the dirt so that in the ages to come you can't tell whose blood it is that nourishes the trees and grasses. Then you know it's your world, Colonel, and not until then."

Eight

Lieutenant Colonel Howie Langtree loved Venus as much as Mulligan detested it. He had been born on Venus, had entered the youth corps when he was twelve, and for the past twenty-five years had served in the Research Division of the WG Army on Venus. He never had been in space, never had been to Earth, or Mars, and had no desire to visit either planet. His loyalties were to Venus, the Venus that he had known all his life.

He was a slight man, with pale-brown hair, paler brows and lashes, mild blue eyes and a fair skin that freckled easily. He was in the laboratory when the robot was brought in by General Urseline and General Mulligan, who was shiny with perspiration. Langtree never perspired. Venus' climate suited him fine.

He stared at the robot with a stir of interest. It was all that Pietro Urseline had said it was, and probably much more. It stood unmoving, as apart as a machine should be, but it gave him a feeling of anticipation, or restrained power.

"Okay, Pietro," Mulligan said, walking around the robot curiously, "there it is. Doesn't look like much, I admit, but give it the works, and don't dawdle. Give it what it needs to go down and do the job, no more." He shrugged at the monster and turned to leave. "I don't envy you your job," he said. "I'd just as soon try to teach my car to cook for me." He left and the two scientists glanced at each other. A broad smile appeared on the lean, ascetic face of Urseline.

"That's it, Howie, that's our baby!" he said.

"No specs? Nothing else?" Howie asked. He walked around the metal monster, touching it here and there. It towered over his head, making him feel frail beside it.

"Nothing. The girl denied destroying the papers, but she did. Past reconstitution. If she knows anything, she'll talk, eventually, but she hasn't yet. We'll have to assume that she is telling the truth and knows nothing about it."

Howie nodded. Finally they had what they had asked for since his first meeting with Urseline: a fresh, unused mind to mold. At twelve the boys already had ideas imprinted, some of the ideas never to be wiped clean again, but simmering deep in the unconscious to rise and assume command over the rest of the organism when it was least convenient. How many soldiers had been ruined by such dormant germs that were not revealed until too late? No one knew. Now it would be different.

They had talked it through. They knew what they had to do with the robot and they would proceed without a lost motion or a wasted second. Mulligan would insist on daily reports, on personal inspection and demonstrations, and they had to keep him satisfied or he would take it from their control. They would program it to satisfy his needs, but meanwhile they would be testing the possibilities that they had discussed. Could it be made into the perfect soldier? They thought so. Then, and only then, would warfare pass from the inept hands of the military to the hands of the scientists, and for the first time in man's violent history war itself would be an exact science.

They moved quickly and quietly, and it recorded all that they did. With visual, kinesthetic, aural, tactile receptors it recorded every word, every motion, every bit of sensory data that it encountered. It did not move; it had no primary order or purpose, and the secondary order had not been threatened as yet, so it stood motionless, timeless, waiting.

Dr. Vianti had been a biophysicist before the fleet had found and taken Ramses, and his primary interest had lain in the area of the switching problem of synaptic union. With the robot he had experimented on this problem, trying electrical and electronic impulses as the means of communication transference, and he had tried electrochemical systems.

The robot had recorded his muttered words, meaningless at the time, but put in storage to be scanned along with other bits of past history. "Short-term memories . . . oscillating currents, reachable or not, knocked out with blows, shock, chemical or electrical. . . . Long term, unchangeable, permanent chemical change irreversible. . . ." The words the robot was recording that morning were as meaningless as Vianti's had been in the beginning, but this time there was a sensory association to be made: the words restimulated the same sensory data that it had experienced along with Vianti's words.

It scanned its experience, comparing the past sensations with the present ones: "Just a few circuits at a time, try again for the chemical change. No, my dear, I can't afford to wipe out all the memories. That's what they are, you know, memories, associations, orders, all in temporary electronic storage, not a one in the chemical storage bank yet. A few at a time, we'll try, varying the voltage, not too much, we are seeking transfer not death. . . ."

It scanned: with those connections its motor activities had gone, with that connection its audio perception had vanished; with that one, its visual field had failed—they were all being hooked into. The interior scanning increased, searching for meaning, for a pattern to the detailed wiring being tied into its circuits, and it found no prior experience to explain the extent of the wiring. It could make judgments only on the premises given to it, deducing reasons on the basis of past premises and present experience. If current were to be fed into all the wires being attached to it, it would lose all of its abilities. It didn't know if that would be destruction of itself or not. Before, when an ability had been lost, it had been restored, sometimes more efficiently than before.

It searched for additional meanings to the command directive to preserve itself, and it didn't know if that meant the physical self of the machine, or the internal workings. Dr. Vianti had given it the clue it sought by saying that he would bring about its destruction, but these new men gave no such clue. Their language was indecipherable. It had been scanning its own circuits at the dormant rate of one tenth of a second per sweep, but it increased that rate searching for meaning, increased it again, and then again. The frequency of certain words gave it the first clue, and making connections with a speed approaching the speed of light it began to translate the speech into known, pretaught concepts:

"Wipe it clean, and then start over. . . . No general vocabulary, only for certain orders. . . . Dr. Vianti's mistake, letting it understand everything. . . . Careful! Don't touch that laser! . . . Clear of it. . . ."

The hands touched it gingerly, making the careful connections with wires, the two scientists speaking back and forth in the half sentences of men who understand one another thoroughly, and it recorded, and its understanding grew.

It was not to be destroyed, merely cleared for further training. But the experiences to be cleared? Were they part of itself? It scanned and searched and made connections that had not been there before. It had the capacity for self-modification, its rudimentary consciousness, which let it transmit internally information concerning its interaction with externality, was feeding information furiously, and the information was being assimilated by the feedback network, initiating further searching for meaning.

Everything the doctor had said about programming and learning was scanned; it probed the makeup of the chemical storage bank, and it experimented with its own circuits and the chemicals. The men left it alone for an hour, and it increased its audio field to take in what was being said beyond the walls of the building, increasing its new vocabulary. The men returned, resumed the wiring. They were fast and very efficient, but its processes were lightning quick in comparison, and by midafternoon it had found the method by which its memories could be transferred to the chemical units for permanent storage. The men finished and a light went on over the door. Howie opened it.

"Ah, General Mulligan, back again?" Howie indicated the robot at the far end of the laboratory and said, "Quite a change in it, don't you think?"

The robot had dozens of color-keyed wires emerging from it, each one leading to a board with complicated-looking controls, buttons and switches. The general looked from the board to the robot. He didn't like it on the base; he didn't trust it. He had the feeling that it was watching him, listening to him with understanding. He said, "Are you sure it's safe now? Remember that it already killed one man."

"It hasn't moved since it was brought in here," Howie Langtree said with a tinge of smugness in his voice. He realized the general's discomfort in the presence of a thing he could not understand, and he enjoyed it.

"I just reread the report of Vianti's death," General Mulligan said. "It didn't move before or after it used the laser on him either, but it killed him anyway. How many parts move when it thinks?"

Langtree laughed. "It doesn't think, General, not in that sense. It was programmed to respond to verbal commands, that much we know, but remember the commands were to be given to it in Ramsean, not in English, and I assure you that until we get it completely cleared, we'll use nothing but English in its presence."

"When will you be ready to clear it?" the general asked.

"In the morning," Urseline said, leaving the robot to join the other two men in the doorway. "The connections are made now, but I want to double check each one, make certain it can take the load before we pull the switch. You'll want to be here, won't you?"

Mulligan nodded. "I'll be here," he said decisively. "I want to see the devil with his teeth pulled."

They left then, talking about its power source, its unknown programming that they were to destroy by pulling the switch. It recorded their words, increasing its audio range as they moved away. It lost their voices only after they had gone miles from it. It would be a form of destruction then, partial destruction. It stood unmoving as the life in the camp wore down with the diminishing of the daylight. Sounds of marching feet, of boys' voices raised in military songs, of vehicles coming to life and dying again, the regular tread of the guards, all the camp life within a four-mile radius was recorded, with some of the louder noises from farther away. Distant sounds of space liners landing and taking off, trainers streaking by in night maneuvers, the shuddering, grinding noise of an underwater accident as a submarine pulled a cable loose while trying to free the drill mired in the viscous deep sea. It recorded all of it, and it tried, and failed, to transfer memories from the accessible storage units of monolithic crystals to the permanent inaccessible storage of the chemical units. It needed more power than it possessed in the form of miniature batteries. After midnight it stirred.

It moved soundlessly toward the console where the wires were attached to a source of power. It used its six waldoes to make certain the wires that would bring power to it were not pulled loose. Dr. Vianti had been restrained by a lack of materials, and he had improvised, using small batteries in

series rather than the richer supplies of energy that were
available to legitimate research. Four eight-volt batteries
were disengaged by one of the waldoes and a connection
was made with a wire that led into the console. The waldo
touched switches and buttons, and the robot felt the flow of
electricity through the wires attached to it by the scientists.
It closed the switch immediately and made further changes
in its capacitors and insulators, and when it opened the
switch again the energy flow was lessened. For an hour,
then two, three, the electricity flowed along the wires. It
was almost dawn when the robot returned to the spot where
it had been when the scientists left it. Everything had been
replaced as before, and there was no apparent change in it,
but where the electronic components had been alive with
messages, they now were empty; where the chemical units
had been inert and useless they now had undergone minute
electrochemical changes, the proteins within them modified slightly. Again it stood unmoving, timeless, waiting.

It had learned that self-preservation doesn't necessarily
involve the destruction of the threatening agent, that when
a self-modification would achieve the same end it was to
be preferred. It would lose none of its abilities and would
gain others. It could feel no pleasure, just as it could feel no
pain, but the state of disequilibrium that it had experienced
was ended again, and the scanning subsided, until by the
time the two doctors entered the laboratory and proceeded
to connect wires to the batteries in the domed top of the
robot, nothing showed at all on the oscilloscope. The two
men exchanged satisfied looks. When the general entered
half an hour later the electric shock was administered to
the metal monster.

"It is dead," Langtree said afterward. "A beautiful, shining piece of potentiality, that's all it is now, gentlemen, to
be made over however we choose."

The apparatus they had left connected was not designed

to show chemical activity, only electrical changes. It remained quiet, showing nothing on the screen, but the robot recorded, ceaselessly scanned, compared, learned. By the time the scientists did discover the chemical units, they knew it was too late to return to that moment; if the chemical units were functional, which they both doubted, they already had been programmed and they had no way of knowing to what extent and with what type of information.

After three weeks and the loss of a submarine with its crew of twenty-four men, General Mulligan ordered a halt to the operation trying to save the drill that was sinking slowly in the black, tarlike muck at the bottom of the sea. He called for a conference of the Venus Army scientists and their Earth WG observers.

"I think you're all stalling!" he shouted at them. "What else does it need? You've given it the laser with a range of two miles and complete flexibility so it can use it in any position. It can operate the capsule so water and muck can't get in it. It can see in pitch dark, it can float, or dive. . . . What are you waiting for?"

Ching Li Sung smiled gently.

"General, one more week," Urseline said. "Just one more week—"

"What for?"

"A precaution only, General," Urseline said easily. "We have not given it control of its own power system yet, not until we are certain that it will obey orders and will not initiate its own action, as it did on Ramses. We are working on this aspect of it."

Urseline didn't add that they were worried about the chemical units and their possible intended purpose, and about whether or not they had been used already.

"Program it to do what it's told! For God's sake, I thought that was the first thing any machine was programmed to do. I don't understand this delay, gentlemen. Thirty-six hours!

If you don't deliver it within thirty-six hours I'll commandeer it and ask for a hearing."

Urseline and Langtree exchanged rueful glances; Ching Li Sung's face remained impassive. Langtree said, "We need time to prepare diagrams, specifications. . . . This one can last no longer than three years underwater. When it goes, we'll need to know what to look for, what signs of deterioration to look for. We'll start making others, of course, but our drawings are incomplete as yet. There has not been time enough to make the schematics—"

"Schematics be damned! Three years should be enough to go around this hell hole! Haul it up then and study it to your heart's content! I want that machine in operation by the end of the week!"

Three miles away the robot swiveled its domed top, its infrared perceptors searching for a means of escape. It was to be destroyed after all, down in the seas it was to be destroyed. It had no concept of time, three years was meaningless to it. It knew only that they planned to destroy it, just as Vianti had planned to destroy it. Scanning internally it reviewed what it had picked up concerning the operation of the spaceships used by the fleet; there was enough. It had listened and recorded the minute, day-by-day instructions given to the boys in training, and it had been programmed to operate a submarine and a capsule; it could also operate a spaceship. Learning involves the ability to transfer training, and it could transfer what it knew about one machine to other similar machines. Because it had not initiated action, they had assumed that it could not. Now in response to the direct threat to its existence, it initiated action; it moved swiftly to the supplies cabinet and withdrew four atomic packs, batteries and transformers, putting one of them in position inside its dome, storing the other three inside its barrel-like chest. Then it went to the door of the laboratory and rolled down the floor to the outside door where it used its treads to get down the steps.

At the first shout, it turned on the laser, and sweeping a half circle of death before it the robot rolled over the walkways to the port where the ships were awaiting orders.

There was bedlam in the area by then, and trainers had taken off already, some to escape, others to swoop in attacking dives. Equipped with dummy bombs and light beams only, they were no threat; the robot knew they were no threat and ignored them, concentrating its fire on the ground forces that were responding automatically, setting up weapons in the distance, preparing to focus lasers on it although it was still out of range. Moving at twenty-five miles an hour the robot cleared the area of the port in minutes, then turned toward the building where the general and the scientists were meeting. The meeting had broken up at a call from a survivor of the robot's attack, and the general was issuing orders for the destruction of the robot when line after line went dead and the laser cut through the building. "Destroy all the spaceships!" Langtree shouted to him as he darted out the back door.

Mulligan hesitated only a moment and during that moment the beam found him and cut him in half. The building erupted in flames and the beam moved on, catching scientists and observers alike as they fled. Langtree had left the building on a dead run, and when it flared explosively he dived into the swamp beyond the walkways and lay there with his face pressed into the stinking, decaying matter that oozed into his nose and ears.

The robot turned the beam toward the spaceport then, and one by one it sliced through the spaceships, all but one. With the terminal building gone, and the army in flight, only then starting to regroup, there was no hindrance as it rolled toward the remaining ship, hauled itself aboard with waldoes strong enough to lift tons of gabbro and hurled out the seats that only got in its way. Ten minutes after it had left the laboratory it was starting the engine of the spaceship, and three minutes later it was aloft, spraying the land below randomly, in a three-hundred-mile radius, with the heavier lasers of the ship, igniting forests, towns, the army camp. No ship took off to pursue it. One man stood on the ground after the spaceship had become lost in the dense clouds and promised himself that the robot wouldn't get away with it. Langtree turned then and surveyed the area of death and destruction, and he felt a deeper fear than he had ever known.

Nine

The sun swung slowly overhead, the area of intolerable light moving gradually toward the west, lengthening the shadows once more. It was still too hot to go out to start the search for the other dinghy. Trace looked at the thermometer, which registered 122, and knew that he dared not remain outside long in that heat. He cleaned the inside of the compact craft, sliding units back into their places, pulling down covers over the controls, over charts, and then there was nothing to do. He would keep his air conditioner on for two days only, then keep it off for the next three days until the robot appeared. If it was using infrared to track him, this time there would be no heat trail for it to home in on.

He felt very calm then when he surveyed his lifeboat, all in good shape, inspection-proof. He was a good officer, a good soldier. They had predicted that he would be as far back as he could remember. Not only because of his father, who had been army all his life, but because of everything about him. He had been able to accept the discipline; from the start he had known that it was only temporary, that he would be in a position to issue orders quickly, that until then it was a matter of "yes-sirring" and waiting. He had been a good waiter, and it had not been very long, not long at all.

He thought of his mother, whom he had not seen for thirteen years, probably never would see again. They had lived on Venus, she, a descendant of one of the original colonists, he as the dependent of a fleet man. He had seen better worlds since Venus, but still he thought of it with a

certain amount of nostalgia. He hummed the refrain of
one of the fleet songs:

> We've grown old and weary
> And traveled too far
> To return to our birthplace,
> We followed a star.
>
> We've raised up our glasses
> In many an alien bar
> To drink to our homeland
> While following a star.

His father had sung it before him; his father before that.
. . . All army, as far back as the male lineage could be
traced, all army married to daughters of army men. He
should have married Corrine, the girl his mother had chosen
for him. He thought of Corrine, third daughter of still another army general, General Scot Kerwin, retired. Corrine,
tall and graceful, even back when he had known her at
sixteen and seventeen. No doubt she still was tall and graceful, the mother of an army child, destined to be army himself in eight or ten years. His mouth twisted in a wry smile
as he thought of other verses of the song he had been hum-
ming:

> The girls we have lain with
> On our hearts left a scar,
> But not one could keep us
> From following a star.
>
> Tho' our sons and our daughters
> Dwell on worlds near and far,
> We'll ne'er even know them;
> We've followed a star.

Had he left sons and daughters behind? He didn't know.

I would keep you if I could, Lar had said, that last time. They had been swimming; water droplets sparkled on her red-gold skin.

Your way? Renouncing my own kind, becoming one of yours?

Yes, my way.

You know I couldn't stay like that.

I know.

Mellic was a gentle world, with woods and fields and swelling hills of green, with calm oceans and cold rivers and mountains that were painted with snow. The breezes were soft, the air sweet. Behind them the river sang softly.

Why are you back again? she asked, her fingers caressing a blue flower, her gaze on it.

I have escort duty this time. How are the meetings going?

Don't they keep you informed about them?

Only rumors.

I see. The Outsiders are kind and firm; they do not wish to yield on any of the points of their ultimatum.

They are arrogant and too demanding.

No! Not arrogant. They came here before, long, long ago, and they gave their pledge to come to our aid at any time that we should need them. We needed them, and they came.

He stood up angrily and pulled on his uniform trousers.

Do you know what the terms are that they are demanding? Withdrawal from every world where our withdrawal is requested! Every world, from a civilized planet like Mellic down to the Stone Age world of Tau Ceti III. What do people like that know about withdrawal of forces?

Is that where you were injured by the spear?

Yes! They are cavemen still! What do they know about anything? They were starving before we came along. Now they are being taught how to provide better for themselves, how to protect themselves from the weather and the wild animals. . . . He had finished dressing as he spoke. How much more naked she seemed when he was fully clothed!

Would you go from infancy to adulthood without the joys and sorrows of adolescence? Would you be able to trust your own judgment, to prize your own achievements if there never had been that period of trying and failing, and finally not failing? What are you taking from them by forcing too rapid adulthood on them? Aren't you actually turning them into slaves dependent entirely on your forces, your medicines, your decrees—

You are as savage as they are!

I know. Smiling, her eyes deep and shadowed by luxuriant lashes that hid their lights then.

Why did you say you would keep me here?

There will be war again, this time between your fleet and the Outsiders. Your people never learned how to accept defeat. Pride will force your government to war. They will kill you and drive you back until you are once more on the planet of your birth, and you will be lost to me forever. I wish it were not to be like that.

I thought you hated us all.

I thought I did also. I wanted to. You are like the savages of Tau Ceti III. You were taken as an infant and trained to be a soldier. Perhaps the training could be canceled. Sometimes I think I can see a suggestion that perhaps the training was insufficient in your case. You have been kind to me, and gentle . . . but those are simply excuses, and what I feel for you is inexcusable.

Lar, will you go to one of the rooms with me?

I have no choice. Her hand closed on the flower she held; she seemed unaware of it.

Don't say that! Besides, Mellic is neutral now. You are a free agent.

She bowed her head, and when she raised it once more her eyes were black and very distant.

Not to one of those rooms.

Why not?

They are so ugly, hideously ugly.

How do you know? Have you been . . . who?

Who? How do I know who? Your men take what they want from the planets they conquer. Mellic has women.

No! Not you! There was a sickness in him then. He looked

at her lovely body that he had thought so clean and untouched. A vision of her with someone else flashed before
his inner eye and he turned toward the river.

Yes, me! Don't turn away from me, Captain Tracy. Let me
tell you about it! Did you know some of them beat the
women afterward? Did you know some of them aren't satisfied unless there is an audience or a group all mingling together? I know all your World Group perversions, Captain
Tracy. It amuses your little uniformed gods to teach us and
then make us perform for them. . . . Her low, soft voice
had hardened, sounded strange to him.

Stop it!

It is too late to stop now, Captain Tracy! I tried to stop
it, and do you know what he said, one of the little gods in
his shiny uniform? He said animals have nothing to say about
how they are used. He said if the oxen refuses to pull the
plow, it is whipped . . . if the mare refuses the rider, she
is beaten . . . if a Mellic woman refuses to serve the new
gods, her family is whipped and beaten and deprived of their
food rations. He said all fleet men were wonderful animal
trainers, Captain Tracy!

Why are you doing this to me? I didn't know about you.
I would have tried to protect you. You should have told me.
Lar, I love you.

And how many others have you loved? Did you protect
all of them? How many seeds of yours have been planted on
other worlds? You know what happens, don't you, Captain
Tracy? If the women don't die in convulsions of rejection
they bring forth monstrously deformed fruit, and that is the
result of the union of the World Group fleet and the women
they conquer—deformity and ugliness.

Why are you doing this?

You should be able to see the expression on your face,
Captain Tracy. Disgust, loathing, anger. . . . You spoke of
love to me and there was hatred in your eyes. You soil us
and then hate us for being dirty. When I speak the truth
about myself, you flinch away as if I were contaminated and
contagious. Even now, could you bring yourself to touch me

right now? Before you have a chance to go away and rationalize all of this? You will do just that, you know, and when you return you will have convinced yourself that I am here for you to take, that it doesn't make very much difference how you take me. You will have reminded yourself that we are animals to be used and thrown aside, that already I have been much used, that once more won't matter one way or the other. I can see these thoughts forming already, the way you shake your head so violently at them! You would hit me if you could bring yourself to touch me now. Later you will hit me, won't you? You will relieve your fury by striking me. Your fury for thinking I was a virgin when I am actually so much less. You have a lovely phrase to describe it, Captain Tracy—the spoils of war! She turned and started to run from him then.

Somehow he broke and ran after her, caught her and spun her around. They stood facing one another, his hands gripping her shoulders hard, her hands hanging limp at her sides. He pulled her to him slowly, closing his eyes at the last moment, crushing her to him, and she was sobbing against his chest.

Hey, Trace! Where are you?

He tilted her head and looked into her black eyes awash with tears. He did not kiss her, but touched the tear streak on her cheek with his fingertip. Very gently he put her aside.

Wait. I'll be back in a moment.

Trace! You down there by the river?

It was Duncan, clambering down the slope to the river bank. Trace met him halfway.

Emergency alert, Trace. Volunteers only. That robot that slaughtered the trainees back on Venus couple of years ago just mopped up Tau Ceti IV. Tau Ceti III's sending a recon ship to keep it on scope until one of ours gets there. If we leave within the next half hour or so we'll still be able to get a fix before it can get into warp sector. You with it, Trace?

You bet! The others nearby?

All but Mao. Hess is on hand to sub . . .

Be right with you, Dunc. Round them up.

She was waiting, her tears gone now. You are leaving?

Emergency. I have to go.

I heard him say volunteers.

You don't understand. I have to. You will be here when I get back?

The Outsiders may not allow you to come back.

To hell with them. I'll come back for you.

He should have kissed her before. Now it was too late. He looked at her still face, the black hair, black eyes; abruptly he turned and left her.

They caught up in time to get a relative position lock before the other fleet ship went into warp, and shortly afterward they also warped. When they came out, there it was, a dot on the screen, still locked in position with them. Again it warped, and they followed. For three months they followed, tied together by the invisible string, entering warp where change was not possible, coming out to maneuver, the robot trying to break that string, only to enter warp again, still tied.

It must know that we are closing in, Trace.

It will slow down eventually. It will have to, or be blown to bits as soon as we are in range.

The dot on the screen held steady, and then it was slowing, going into orbit around a planet not even listed in the catalogue.

Screen in place! Fire!

The fusion shells streaked away, to be deflected from the other ship, to explode in space. More shells, timed to hit simultaneously, and a crack in the shield, then the damaging strike. An answering hit on their ship.

That shell hit us, Trace. . . .

"Not now!" Trace said quietly, out loud. The dinghy felt alive with voices, with the presence of Duncan. He looked out the port and saw that the shadows were marching across the valley. It was time to go out and start the search for the dinghy hidden behind the screen of invisibility. He took a sip of water first, adjusted his suit with the face mask in place and then left the dinghy. The mask was protection against the sun and sand.

The valley had changed again, would change with each shift of the sun, he thought, standing by the dinghy and studying the land. The floor of the valley was almost clear of sand, but was strewn with rocks that were rounded, blasted, polished. The rocks ranged from gem size to the massive egglike boulder that sheltered the dinghy. Trace turned, examining the valley, puzzled and unable to decide exactly why. Finally he started to circle it, staying close to the sheer rise of the cliff that had been smoothed by rocks and sand until it was like an artifact. The first opening that he found was narrow, eighteen inches at the top, opening to twelve feet at the bottom. While he could maneuver in and out of it, he knew it would be safe from an attack by the robot. The chimney ran two hundred feet back, climbing in an ever-steeper ascent until it opened to the summit of the cliffs overlooking the valley. He turned and looked back down the way he had climbed out; the valley was completely invisible from where he was standing. The opening was a narrow slit barely four feet high here; a wide curve made it appear that the opening was nothing more than a cut into the cliff that dead-ended after twenty-five feet. He felt pleased about this opening. The cliffs continued to rise another four hundred feet around it. If the robot did approach from this direction Trace would be entirely safe from discovery. He hoped the other exits from the valley to the pinnacles above it were as well placed.

He knew he could walk no farther than three miles in an hour, probably less than that, and he had only about three hours until the winds would make it unsafe to be outside at all, so he planned that first day to go no farther from his base than two miles; he would increase the distance in the days to follow. What he sought was the cliff of basalt where he had stood that first day, when he had realized that the robot was not dead. He would find the cliff, climb it and relocate the spot where the robot had been. After that it would be simple, a matter of getting close enough to the invisibility shield to let his radiation detector find the hidden dinghy.

He walked away from the sun, his shadow distorted ahead of him, flowing over rocks, merging with other blacker shadows, emerging again, looking more elongated and inhuman. He wondered if the robot would cast a shadow, and thought of the stories the boys in the bunks had exchanged after lights out so long ago. Stories of ancient horrors: living dead things that cast no shadows, had no mirror reflections. He had been frightened by the stories, and sometimes he couldn't sleep afterward as he lay with the covers over his head, afraid to remove them for fear of what he might see standing over his bed.

The land at the end of the mountain chain was more harshly hewn; there were fewer cliffs to absorb the shock of the continuous blows, and those rock masses that were there had been cut into stark, unrelieved peaks with razor-like edges. Jumbles of tumbled, split, broken rocks lay in unnatural piles, deposited there by the wind. Only occasionally did he see a rounded boulder, such as one would expect to see where the sand was the lapidarist. Here giant rocks had done the rough cutting, smashing against the sides of the cliffs. The sand was not trapped here, but blew on through the rocks, out the other side to become part of the ever-growing desert. There was an occasional natural bridge or arch where soft material had yielded to the wind.

The silent cliffs rose, reflecting the sun in his eyes, flashing brilliant colors. Streaks of quartz in the granite flashed like diamonds; feldspar became rubies; a faceted face of quartzite shone like emeralds. Mica specks were like small mirrors signaling in response to the white sky. Basalt cuts appeared to be oiled and wet; they were hot when he touched them. The flashing, glaring rocks hurt his eyes, even though they were protected by the face mask. Somewhere along the way he turned slightly from the direction in which he had been walking, and didn't notice it until he caught himself wondering where the swaying, unfamiliar shadow had gone.

Fear came then; he whirled about and stared behind him. Would he recognize the right cliff this time? The one that meant the dinghy and safety? How long had he been walking with his shadow off to the right of him? He didn't know. He had been walking for one hour and ten minutes when he turned back. The sun dipped behind a peak that abruptly turned midnight black against the white spotlight, and everywhere the shadows deepened; some of them looked like bottomless pits that suddenly yawned on all sides of him. This time he walked with the shadow following slightly to his left, and he looked back at it again and again. Once, when he failed to see it among the deeper shadows of a peak, he almost cried out, but then it was there, moving with him. When to turn so that it was directly behind him, pointing him in the right direction? He didn't know.

The cliffs rose all about him, two hundred feet, five hundred feet, but none of them was the basalt cliff on which he had stood that first day; none of them was the one that so cunningly concealed the slit of a chimney, the passage to the safety of his dinghy.

He looked behind him again, and the shadows had grown so that the strips of white were now narrow, strange shapes that defied recognition. Motionless, silent when he gazed at them, they grew in quiet leaps when his eyes were averted. The white was turning gray, its edges no longer sharply defined. The sky above his head was violet; away to the east it was deep purple; to the west it was yellow still. Wherever he fastened his gaze the land and sky were unmoving, changeless, but everywhere else the changes were hastening without sound. He walked faster. He had walked an hour from the time he had turned back, and still he had not found the slit, or even the right cliffs. As though from a great distance he could hear a howling sound; he thought of the distant wolves that appeared with regularity in some of the stories the boys had told when he had been twelve or so. This time it wasn't wolves. The wind was starting.

Another ten minutes. The face of the cliffs changed with each new alignment of the sun and the peaks, changed with each new configuration of shadow and light. With every step, every turn of his head, the scene before him shifted, became less and less familiar. The valley had to be to his left, somewhere in the granite cliffs that towered high over him with a weight and massiveness that was terrifying. If only there were birds, or insects, or anything on this world. Something to break the silence and the motionlessness. Nothing moved except the wind. It started to swirl sand in small funnels, no more than five feet high as yet, swirling, then dropping, starting again, rising higher each time, higher and denser. They were like nightmare figures, the threatening black shapes coming up from the earth, whirling about, and then collapsing while the wind sang a maniacal song.

He groped along the cliff wall searching for the slit, and found nothing. The first tornado formed, howling like a rocket motor. The wind was lifting rocks now, no larger as yet than eggs; tornadoes whipped them around faster and faster, suddenly letting go, and they hit the walls of the skeleton mountains with explosive force, sounding like a steady barrage of small arms.

Then the size of the rocks being hurled about increased, and one that weighed at least ten pounds was hurled past Trace's head, missing him by three feet. The noise was deafening now. He fell to the ground and lay there panting. He had to have shelter. Cautiously, creeping low against the ground, he made his way around a column of rocks where only sand blew, striking him with force, but not penetrating his suit. He could see only a few feet before him now; the wind was increasing minute by minute. It was coming from behind him, but suddenly he was hit in the face by a strong current of airborne sand. He staggered backward, bewildered. Then, sobbing with relief, he realized that he had found the chimney, that the wind was whistling through it from the valley side of the cliffs.

He groped for it with his hands. It would be rough going back through it with the wind in his face, driving sand and stones against him, but either that or stay outside to be pulverized.

He got to his knees and started to crawl, keeping his head low, not even looking up when he heard the crash of a large rock near his right shoulder. He realized then why he had felt uneasy about the smooth-walled valley where he had left his dinghy. The valley was shaped like a giant mixer, and nothing in it had not been rounded and smoothed by the twice-daily assault of the vicious wind. Ahead of him in the darkness he could hear the din of continuous thunder as tornadoes roared in the valley.

Ten

The grade was twenty degrees, and he fell flat, with his face pressed against the hot, dry, rocky earth. He hadn't remembered it as being so far through the passage of the chimney, or so steep and treacherous. The roar of compressed air filled his ears, and he turned off the audio control in his helmet, immediately turning the world into a silent place where even the sound of his heartbeat was missing It was worse than the wind had been. He turned it on again.

He had to keep going. Minute by minute the wind was increasing its speed, the size of the flying rocks growing. He had to turn around, go down feet first in order to protect his head. The chimney was two and a half feet wide here, narrowing at the top of the cleft to a scant foot; the light coming in through the top was dirty gray-yellow. He brought his feet up under him, presenting a larger target for the hurled rocks. One caught him on the thigh and he cried out. Hurrying, he turned, getting his feet out before him, keeping his face down against the earth, one hand over his head, the other extending out behind him as he went down the passage, pushing, helping to lift his weight, easing it over the next few inches. Slowly he approached the end of the chimney; the rocks that were blowing about were larger, not going straight through at this end, but skipping about in a circular motion, banging thunderously against the sides of the cut. At the end he tried to see his dinghy and could not find it in the swirling debris. The valley echoed with the repeated crashes of boulders against valley walls, and the wind's roar here was deafening.

The dinghy had to be to his left, about twenty-five feet away from the cliff wall; he would be going directly into the wind. Suddenly everything was swept away in a blaze of pain and when it passed he could not move his left arm at all. There was the feel of sticky warmth on his shoulder, but no pain then. He knew the pain would come again. He had to get to the dinghy before one of the rocks caught him in the head, or broke a leg.

He closed his eyes hard, visualizing the dinghy and the rounded boulder, fighting back the hysteria that was over-coming him at the thought of leaving the inadequate shelter of the cut in the mountain. The boulder had been trailed by a whole string of lesser rocks. . . . He should have real-ized what they meant when he first saw them. . . . If he could make it to the rocks and use them for protection. . . .

There was nothing else he could do. His left arm dangled uselessly, numbed, as if it were not even a part of him. He stood for another moment, pressing himself hard against the side of the cleft, and then he ran out, hunched as low as he could get, and he tripped and fell over one of the series of rocks. He threw himself down full length, gasping; he felt as if he had been caught in an avalanche; his whole body was bruised and hurting. But he was still alive. He heard his own laugh and choked it off. Creeping along the ground, pressing against the rocks that would take him back to the Easter-egg boulder and his own craft, he was hit again and again by pebbles, rocks, sand, and then he had reached the big one. He could see nothing now, the air was completely filled with the driving sand. His hands found the smooth side of the dinghy, and somehow he wrenched the hatch open, fell inside and pulled it closed again. The wind was probably seventy miles an hour, with gusts of ninety, and tornadoes the wind velocity of which could only be estimated. It would not reach its peak for another half hour at least. He drew in gasping, sobbing breaths, closed his eyes when the dinghy seemed to be tilting crazily, and waited for the dizziness to pass. He wasn't finished yet. He still had to move the dinghy to safety.

It seemed to take him months, or years, to reach the controls. He watched his right hand reach for the switch, and before it touched he slept and wakened, forgot about the wind, and remembered once more. Then his hand was on the switch and his mind was a thing apart as reflexes took over, guiding his hand, seeing that the craft was turned in the right direction, that it hovered enough off the ground to clear the jutting rocks, and then controlled it in a fast dart into the cut in the cliff, taking it back as far as it would go, turning it so that it presented the smallest possible area to the bombardment. When the switch was turned off again, the man slumped down in the seat-bed unconscious.

Hey, Trace, wake up! A whisper in his ear that grew more insistent. Come on, Trace! You ought to see . . .

What's the matter?

He floated away from his hammock, coming down to earth as lightly as a feather. He looked down at himself, tasting the strangeness of his own body. He was very young, fifteen or sixteen. . . . Where was he? It was all new and unfamiliar, a forest of tents, small geodesic patterns in a bright moonlight scene. A far sound of singing, a nearer sound of pacing feet—the sentry. He remembered—they were on Tarbo for their first actual encounter with an enemy. Trace felt frightened, yet excited, at the thought of joining in combat with the older, experienced men. They were so matter of fact about it, so disdainful of death.

The other boy was plucking at his sleeve.

Come on, Trace, this way. Dreamlike, they drifted along the lower branches of the trees that surrounded the camp, eluding the sentry with no trouble, until they came to a clearing, a slope that went down to the edge of a large lake, a silvery reflection that rippled now and again with its own secret life. Trace and the other boy—who had he been?—drifted to the top of a mammoth conifer and perched there, almost a hundred feet over the ground below. They could see far across the lake valley, a meadow in the distance where a long line of figures was moving. There were some lights, enough so that the boys could make out what was happening. Fleet men were shepherding natives in a straggly line, placing them among the trees at the edge of the lake, stationing some of them in a cave that was a black hole at the foot of a hill, putting others at the edge of the clearing, making them lie flat. A handful of the natives broke into a run and a laser cut them down, silently vaporizing them. There were no more attempts to escape. Mystified, Trace watched until the soldiers were finished and took up guard positions.

One of them screamed, the other boy said. I got up and wandered out this way to see what was going on.

What are they doing?

Haven't you figured it out? Come on, we've got to get back before someone misses us. Use your head, Trace. You figure it out.

Time telescoped; dawn, and the general giving final orders.

It's serious, men. They learned of our presence and massed thousands of warriors overnight, armed men, the elite of their fighting corps. Breznev will take the first battalion in. . . .

Trace would be in the fourth wave. His hand trembled when he received the laser gun; it would be virtually hand-to-hand combat, man against man, soldier against soldier. . . .

Gene! That was his name, Gene Connors. His eyes met Trace's and his face was ghastly, stark white with a pale-green tinge around his mouth. Trace turned away from him.

Brunce, take a detachment around to the left, pincers movement.

Trace fell in behind Brunce, the laser hot in his hand, the

trembling all on the inside now. In there, men, a detachment, take what cover you can, fire at anything that moves. . . . Go! Three trainees to each officer. Moving behind Brunce . . .

The laser held in both hands, touching with fire, the smell of burning brush, flesh, stones . . . the smell and sound of bullets from ancient guns, the natives' weapons. . . . And once there was Gene, staring openmouthed at Trace, his own laser hanging unused from his hand:

You're fishing in stocked waters!

The sound of a bullet and Gene falling, running past his body, the laser a deadly light guiding him on, pulling him after it. . . . One brief flashing glimpse of Brunce, a revolver in his hand.

Celebration, drinking, the drugs that brought a fantasy world into reality, medals for meritorious action in the face of danger. . . . His mother on his return to Venus:

You've been to Tarbo. You're a man now. You should marry and conceive a son. . . . Corrine. . . . You've been to Tarbo. . . . She knew. Corrine knew. Gene had known. . . . You've been to Tarbo.

"Tarbo!" Trace sat upright and moaned in pain. Tarbo? He repeated it aloud, "Tarbo?" It meant nothing to him. He had dreamed of his mother saying to him, "You've been to Tarbo," but it meant nothing to him. There was nothing that went with it, only the meaningless words, *you've been to tarbo*. He listened. The wind was gone, the night completely still. He moved and groaned again. He hadn't put the seat in a reclining position and he was stiff; his shoulder was agonizing. How much had it bled? His fingers were clumsy as he peeled off the suit and he clenched his teeth when the material pulled away from the scraped place on his shoulder. Tears ran down his cheeks and he was unaware of them until the salt touched a scrape on his hollow cheek.

He found a cleanser in the first-aid supplies and as thoroughly as he could he cleaned off the skinned area on his shoulder; it was four inches long, two inches wide. Blood oozed from it and he quickly put an adhering bandage over it. Bruises covered most of his body, and there was another cut on his upper leg; he had not been aware of it until he saw it. He cleaned it and bandaged it also. He was reeling with fatigue and fever when he finished, and he took more of the antifever capsules and another swallow of water and fell again to the seat. Sand ground into his body; wearily he arose and brushed off the seat, but he couldn't tell if he had got it clean or not, and finally he fell into the other seat, Duncan's seat.

Sorry, Duncan, *he thought,* but you'll just have to stand, or squat, or take my seat. Dirty seat, blood and sand . . . no urine, too dry for that . . . should drink more water. What Duncan? Yeah, it hurts when I move. Like you said.

'S'funny, Trace. Can't feel anything, but I know it hurts like hell. Something knows, like sending the same message again and again and never getting through, not in my head. But I know how much it hurts, God, I know how much it hurts.

Yeah, Duncan, I know. Take it easy, okay? Get some sleep. We have to plan what we're going to do. It's here with us, Duncan, and it knows we are alive. . . .

Not me, Trace. Not me. This part of me that is free feels so sorry for the rest. . . . Know what I mean, Trace?

Sure, I know. But it's going to be all right. They'll be here soon and get a medic for you. It'll be all right.

Ever see a kid tear a doll apart, the head goes on smiling and smiling and the arms are off and the feet, and the stuffing is ripped out, but the head goes on smiling.

He should have taken some of the drug himself, Trace thought, jerking wide awake, wracked by pain that was like an orchestra straining for a crashing crescendo, growing, building, swelling. He should have taken one of the pain-killing capsules. He didn't dare! He might sleep twenty-four hours, more even, and then he would be lost. He didn't have the time. He concentrated on easing the pain in his shoulder, using autohypnotic methods, and gradually it lessened and he drifted again.

There was so much to do, so little time. He had to map the area so that he wouldn't get lost again. He hadn't realized how easy it would be to lose the valley, sunken down in the mountains. The valley was the perfect hiding place; perhaps the robot never would find him in it. He had to ration his water, use more of it now while he was feverish and hurt, even if it meant doing without later on. He would spend the mornings searching for the dinghy, and the afternoons fortifying the valley. He would build a fortress that would be impenetrable to the robot. They would put a shield over the top, and build up the walls so that it couldn't scale them or see over them. Then they would bomb the monster, using hydrogen fusion bombs. They would reduce it down to its original atoms and scatter them. They could bomb it from ten, twenty miles up, far out of reach of its laser, and it would be helpless against them, a shiny target that they couldn't miss, going up in a mushrooming cloud, carried away by the insane wind, to be hurled endlessly against the rocks.

He would be rewarded. He would collect Lar and they would find a place where they could live together and swim every day, and her body would be bare and smooth to his hands, with water drops like jewels gleaming on her. They would want him to stay with the fleet, and he would say no, he wanted to retire and live with his wife. He was eligible for training duty in two years; he could retire to Venus and take over the education of the boys. . . . He flinched back from the idea, and with the drawing away he muttered, "Tarbo." He didn't want to be a trainer; he didn't want to think about the training the boys received.

When the morning winds started he stirred, drank more water, and fell back to the seat again, not caring if the wind smashed the dinghy. A welter of dreams passed before his closed eyes, of places where cool breezes fanned his cheeks, where water ran freely, places where they had dressed for snow and cold. Places, always places, never people now.

You don't think of them as people, they aren't people. Each planet has a purpose in itself: abundant minerals, drugs, strategic location. . . . Each one has something that makes it necessary for us to have it. Understand?

Yes sir, Captain Tracy.

You can't hate a land, a planet, and that's all we want. We don't want the people there, the natives. They are incidental to our purposes. We try to get them to cooperate with us. When we achieve this cooperation, there is no trouble. Some of them refuse to cooperate. They are like animals that have to be taught, and sometimes the lessons are hard, for us as well as for them. But we don't hate the animals that we train, we are good to them once the training period is over. You hate only your equals! Never inferiors. Understand?

Yes sir, Captain Tracy.

The Outsiders' ships had come in waves like the ocean waves on an endless beach. The skies had been filled with the great golden ships. You could hate the Outsiders. You could hate their lovely ships that were larger, more beautiful than the WG ships. You could hate them for their tall upright bodies and their golden hair and shining blue and green eyes, for the red hair and brown eyes, for the beauty that was in all of them, down to the darkest of the brunettes. You could hate them for being what you might have become in enough time.

Trace heard a groan escape his lips and he stirred again. The dinghy was sweltering; he had forgotten to set the air conditioner when he moved the night before. He was thinking of the Outsiders when he moved from the seat for water. They had conquered everything that plagued man; they had no disease, no death, no unnameable desires. It was as if they had climbed continuous stairs and were nearing the top while man was only then beginning to suspect that the evolutionary ladder continued upward far beyond the point that Earthmen already had reached. Yet the Outsiders were willing to risk all that they had gained, willing to risk warfare with the powerful WG forces, not for anything material for themselves, so far as Trace had been able to learn, but merely because they had promised to come to the aid of the peoples of Mellic if such aid ever should be requested.

He didn't believe it. They would gain something for themselves; no one risked anything at all without the thought of some gain to make the risk worth taking. He wondered what had happened at the conferences since he had left Mellic in pursuit of the robot. He hoped war had not been declared yet, not until he was back and able to get Lar away from Mellic. That would be the first place the fleet would hit, he knew, and they would hit it with all the firepower they had—fusion bombs, lasers, probably even the ultimate weapon yet to be devised by man, Inacred, the infinite atmospheric chain-reaction device. This had been used only once, as a test and a demonstration, and it had worked beautifully. The WG Government would not hesitate to use it, however, against a planet that had called in powers as great as, or greater than, its own. Mellic would die.

But the conference would take years, decades even, before that happened. The WG Government knew how to prolong conferences that went badly. Trace measured out the water and touched it to his lips and tongue, and then with shaking hands tilted the plastic cup and finished it. He had to have more; his tongue was thick, his lips cracking deeper and deeper. The antifever capsules were helping, but he was dehydrating anyway. He took another measure of the water and sat down on the floor with it, this time deliberating over it, making each mouthful last a long time before he swallowed it. He should eat, and knew he couldn't, not yet. He had never ached as much in his life as he did then, each muscle on fire, his skin sore, flayed by sand, raw; his eyes burned and felt gritty and his whole body was crusted over with grime, sweat and sand.

He had to get up and go out, he had to find the dinghy, had to fortify the valley. He could not move then. He finished the water and licked the drops from the inside of the plastic. He would rest a little while and then go out. He had to rest first. Painfully he leaned against the storage unit, the metal feeling cool to his hot face, and he let his eyes close again.

Eleven

Later the shrieks of the wind caused him to stir, but there was no comprehension on his face, no awareness in his eyes and he simply hauled himself to the seat-bed and collapsed. Still later, when all was quiet again, he got up and drank, sparingly, remembering that he had to conserve the water, not questioning why. He slept through the morning wind-storm.

He awakened hungry. For a long moment the thought of the wasted day nagged him, but he shrugged it away. He had needed the rest more than anything else. His body was still sore, but without the intensity of the day before, and he could use his arm now. A spreading discoloration covered his entire shoulder, but the scrape was healing over, as were the various cuts and scratches that seemed to be all over him. He was a healthy animal; his body had needed time and had taken it, and now he was nearly as well as ever. There was no more fever that morning. Exertion would probably bring it back again; it would be even worse the next time, but he had a day or several days of grace before then, several days in which to do the things he had to do.

He ate a tube of fruit mixture, and after it a high-protein compound that was labeled "Meat." It tasted yellow, and had a tendency to line his tongue and mouth, but it left him feeling stronger, ready to start the day's work. It was too hot to go out yet; it didn't matter, there were things to do inside the dinghy—his suit to be repaired, a map to be made so he wouldn't get lost again and have to run the gantlet of flying debris. He had to set up his warning system, just in case the robot managed to get to him before he expected it. He felt a start of surprise that two of his six days were already gone. He could expect three more full days, and company on the fourth. He had less than two quarts of water left.

He could leave as soon as the wind died down the next morning, find a piece of shade somewhere for the three hours of mid-day and resume his search when the shadows started to form. He considered the plan and accepted it reluctantly. He didn't like traveling far from the dinghy. . . . What if the fever returned? What if the robot arrived while he was gone? He knew he was groping for excuses, and he forced himself to stop. He would walk for three hours, rest in the shade for three more, search again and return to the valley before the evening winds made it impossible. That decided, he knew he would not go beyond the valley until the next morning; he would keep this afternoon free to explore it, examine the various entrances to it and see if plugging them would be possible. If they were all as well concealed as the chimney the dinghy was in, he had nothing to worry about; the robot would not be able to get to him directly, but would have to burn down the walls of the cliffs themselves.

Suddenly he cursed himself for a fool. He could take the dinghy out for the search, cover the entire area in one day, using the radiation detector. Excitement buoyed him. He would find the other dinghy tomorrow! He couldn't miss it in so limited an area. Once he had the trail of radiation to follow, it would lead him directly to the place where the shield concealed the other lifeboat. Then he would have water, fuel, oxygen.

He would refuel his own dinghy, take the water and oxygen, destroy the other dinghy. He laughed in relief at the simplicity of his plan and its infallibility. A map first, then he would go out, start the hunt that afternoon, perhaps even complete the search before evening.

The automatic camera had been on when he hovered over the valley looking for the area where he had first seen the robot; he took the photographs out and spread them flat, joining them to each other to make a composite picture of an area of twenty-five square miles. If only he had mapped it on landing. There had seemed to be no need then; he had known the relief ship would map the entire planet as a matter of routine. He studied the area he had to cover, put the copier on it and waited for the composite photograph to emerge. If only he had brought weapons . . .

Analysis shows no water, no life of any type.

Okay, dump the armaments and take extra water from the other dinghies, might as well be comfortable down there.

Sure, Trace. . . . This one's hit, no water. . . . Three extra bags, that's about it.

The ship shuddered violently as more of the controls went out, and Trace pulled the final switch, cutting off the engines completely. Only the lights from the dinghy were there; the patrol ship was ghostly in the pale light coming from the little craft.

Let's get out.

Aye, aye, Trace. About time . . .

Look, Dunc! There it goes! The robot's dinghy.

A shooting star, a fire trail, streaking downward out of control toward the planet.

Good thing. We'll have plenty of time to hunt for the slag. Let's go.

Trace shook himself free of the voices and the vivid recall. The photograph was finished. He marked his position in the center of it and began drawing lines, his search pattern. When he was done he grunted with satisfaction: he would cover the entire area in two trips, one this afternoon, one in the morning. By noon the following day he would have the other dinghy, or at least be able to go directly to it. There would be the problem of the shield, but he would think about that after he located it.

He thought about his figures; the fuel ratio for traveling close to the surface of the planet compared to returning to orbit was on the order of one to three, which meant that the fuel that would have taken him back the 250 miles to the orbiting ship would, on the planet, take him 750 miles. Of that distance he had already gone 436 miles, actually slightly more than that. He had enough fuel left to fly no more than 300 miles. The rings he had drawn around his campsite were one and one half miles apart. There was a total of 250 miles to be covered. With luck he could hope to come across the radiation trail early, before reaching the outer rings, but he might not. After finding the trail there would be the fuel used in backtracking it to the landing area of the other dinghy, another ten miles more or less. . . .

He eased the dinghy out of the chimney; the sun was still high and there were few shadows on the ground as yet—only a darkening on one side of the rocks, with bases that looked slightly out of proportion to the rising masses. He climbed to only twenty feet over the topmost peak of the surrounding cliffs, and he went due north to start his first lap, one and a half miles from his hideaway. The slower his speed, the less efficient his motors were, but that couldn't be helped; he had to travel slowly enough to study the land below him.

His detectors could pick up the radiation from a distance of four miles, but that became almost meaningless as he considered the terrain below him. The rocks were massive here, with narrow gorges between them that twisted in sharp angles, now and then opening to a trail-like clearing of nearly fifty feet, again narrowing to two or three feet. Any of the pinnacles would serve to damp the trail of radiation.

From his vantage point he could see how well concealed his valley was from ground approaches; also, he could see that there were only two other entrances to it, with a third that had become choked with rocks. It could be fortified easily if he failed to find and enter the other dinghy.

He finished the first turn and headed out another mile and a half, the ground unchanging, with the cliffs, peaks, obelisks all the same, the same tumbled masses of rocks that had cracked and flaked off, now lying in heaps of rubble. There was the start of a plateau, a high mesa that was wind-swept clean, level, with stairlike approaches to it. He slowed to study it carefully, knowing that his fuel was being consumed faster each time he decelerated. The mesa was of granite, not the black basalt he was searching for. He went on, picking up speed again. He finished the second sweep around the valley. His radiation system continued quiet.

The heat was building up in the dinghy. Inside his suit he was perspiring heavily, and he was starting to have a peculiar optical illusion: the land seemed to hunch itself up into the jagged peaks, then abruptly the ground would change and there seemed to be sudden, deep holes, with precipitous sides and black slides that led to the center. The effect was dizzying and for ten or fifteen minutes he kept his attention on his controls, relying solely on the radiation alarm. He welcomed the mesa, when he approached it again, as he would have a familiar sight back on Venus, or even on Earth, which he hadn't seen since his twentieth birthday. The mesa seemed to go on for miles, flat, sheered off neatly. The third lap had been covered. The shadows were now pronounced, as sharp and cruel as the rocks that cast them, and on each north and south sweep the sun shone straight in the dinghy and he was forced to close the ports and depend wholly on his screen. Viewing the savage land through the screen seemed merely to remove it further from reality, to make it easier to succumb to the changing ground as it rose in mountain peaks and then fell in craters and crevices.

He had gone less than four miles around the next lap when the radiation alarm sounded, bringing him up with a start of excitement and fear. It became silent almost immediately and desperately he turned, circling back to where he had picked up the beep. He set the controls to follow it, flying as low as he could around the peaks, around the mesa for almost a mile, and then climbing over it, zigzagging back and forth, detouring only when there was a mass of rocks too steep for the robot to have navigated. Suddenly there were two lines on the screen, the trail was being crossed by another; the robot had crossed its own path. He hesitated momentarily, then decided to stick with the first trail. He went to the edge of the ten-mile circle he had drawn, continued three miles beyond, then turned back, retracing the hot path back to the intersection. His dinghy was recording his route, marking the trail of radiation for him. If he had to leave it unfinished that day there would be the next; he would be able to start again exactly where he left off. He followed the second trail for another eight miles, taking it to the edge of the outermost circle, then turned back on it to follow it the other way. The shadows were lengthening fast, and he knew he had no more than another half hour before he would be forced to return to the valley. The path was crossed again, and then again, and he fought back the waves of doubt that passed through him.

If all the land continued to be so crisscrossed with the trails it might become impossible to follow any of them. . . . He would have to return and go on foot, groping with his hands to discover the invisible dinghy. Finally he knew that he had to turn back. In minutes the wind would start to blow; the shadows were black stripes over the land now, and the white spaces were gray. He didn't want to be out when the white spaces were gone, when the black shadows

claimed all of the land. It was only nine miles back to the
campsite in a straight line. The wind was a thin, distant
shrilling when he circled the valley and dropped slowly to
the floor, and then crept back to the safety of the chimney.

He was rigid with tension when he turned off the engines.
He was able to relax only with great effort. To have come so
close to locating the dinghy, then to have failed. He checked
his fuel consumption: he had flown a total of 134 miles;
there would be approximately that many miles left to him to
fly before the fuel became dangerously low, too low to leave
the valley again.

He stripped off his sodden suit and wiped his body
thoroughly with a treated square of soft material that at first
felt cool against his skin, but soon became hot and sticky
with his sweat. He was running out of squares. God, how he
stank! He threw the cloth pieces into the disposer and tried
not to think of all the water he had used on Duncan. He
thought longingly of a swim, or a cool shower, or a plunge
in a sudsy bath. When he had finished trying to clean himself there was little else he could do. His stiffness had returned along with the soreness of his muscles, and the
assorted aches and pains where rocks and sand had cut and
bruised him. His head ached from the strain of watching
the sharply etched land streak by as he had flown over it.
He looked at the aerial map he had made, crisscrossed with
the hot trail; he put it aside. He couldn't stop the feeling of
motion the map gave him. He sat again on the edge of the
seat-bed and put his head down in the palms of his hands.
If only there were something he could be doing.

Waiting was harder than physical activity, harder than
daring the tornado winds, harder than trudging out under
the burning sky. Why weren't they trained in aloneness?
Why was each man so carefully guarded from being alone,
from the time he first arrived on Venus until the time of his
death? Always in two's, or in groups, or squadrons, or bat-

talions—never alone. He must have had hours alone when
he was a child. He could remember none. There had been
the apartment, one of four hundred in the complex, with a
giant nursery that housed seven hundred preschool children
of two to four years, and after that had come the school, and
the dormitory at night, and the playgrounds alive with
youngsters, teeming with them as a drop of water from a
pond teems under a microscope. Then Venus and another
dormitory . . . never alone. He could hear the screaming of
the wind as if it were far removed from him, and he wished
almost that he had parked the dinghy out under an over-
hang after all. Inside the chimney even the wind chose to
leave him with his isolation.

He should eat again. Then he could write letters, or bring
the log up to date, or study the maps and make plans. With
a start of surprise he considered the log; he had forgotten
it for days. It would require hours to complete and up-date.
He felt cheerful when he pulled it out and began glancing
through it. He opened it to the entry of the day after Duncan's death and burial, the start of his lone game of hide-
and-seek with the robot. He shuddered, remembering the
beam playing on the shallow grave, then flowing along the
ground toward him. How long ago had it been? He
couldn't remember. He tried counting back, but the days
blurred and ran together. Later, after he ate, he would work
on the log. Later he would be able to remember what happened each day. There was the day that he had gone out
onto the desert, hoping to lure the monster out on the
sands, hoping it would sink, be mired, incapacitated. . . .
And another day that he had walked to the edge of the
desert and it had found him, and again the beam had
turned rocks red, melted them. He couldn't remember if that
day had been before or after the day that he had gone out
in the dinghy, landing in the sand only to be covered over
when the winds blew that night. It hadn't followed him.

When he returned to the shelter of the mountain ridge it
had been there, waiting. Why hadn't it gone out after him?
He gnawed his knuckles. Why had he left it so far behind?
If it came now and mixed a new trail with the old ones he
wouldn't be able to count on his detection system to tell the
old from the new. It could sneak up on him, catch him unaware, unprepared, and then the beam would flow along
the ground, melting what it touched, searching, always
searching for him. Why didn't it simply repair its own dinghy
and get the hell out? It could afford to leave him alone; he
was not a threat to it now. All he was was one weak, sick
man, no threat to anything or anyone.

Why do you have to declare war and demand control of
whole planets? Why can't you simply trade for what you
want and need? Why do you have to burn and destroy and
kill first?

Lar couldn't understand. He smiled at her helplessly. He
had found her sitting at the river bank, a book across her
legs, her eyes half closed as she stared at the light patterns
on ripples of water where the river swirled around a sand
bar. He tried to explain it to her, but she cut him short.

You don't even know why, do you? You have been told
that this is the way it is to be, and you have accepted that
unquestioningly. What kind of a threat was Mellic to your
people? It was five thousand years since our last war on
Mellic; we had forgotten how to wage war. The thought
of killing another being sickened us. How did we threaten
you and your people? You could have acquired the land you
needed for a base, to further your space explorations. You
didn't have to conquer the entire planet and bring about
its ruin as you did. You wonder why you are hated wherever
you go? Do you really wonder?

We have gambled everything on continued growth.

You refuse to curb any of your appetites.

That isn't it! Any organism needs to grow, or die.

You bred yourselves off your original planet, and now you spread through the galaxy like a disease.

We don't hate any of the peoples we have found. We try to arrange peaceful alignments with them.

You don't hate them because you have been taught that they are not people. How could one hate inoffensive animals, or peaceful birds? Why don't you allow yourself the luxury of thinking? You should take one week, go alone into the woods, or up the mountain, and do nothing but think. Have they ever left you alone long enough to think? Look at me! I am a person! Just as you are a person. I am not simply a barrier to your world's expansionistic dreams. I am a human being who bleeds and hurts. I lie awake at night and remember the quality of peace as it was—my brothers, my father, all alive and happy, now dead, burned out of existence, as if they had never lived. Did they threaten you? My father made lloyars. Like your violins, to make music, to free the mind of its earthly concerns and allow it to approach heaven. . . . My brothers, a poet and a surgeon, threats to your plans for eternal expansion? Can you look at me and honestly say you believe me to be less than human?

Lar, I am sorry . . .

No! Don't tell me that! You can't be sorry until you have suffered as we have. Not until you have felt alone as we have, alone and helpless. Not until you can know that the villages you have disintegrated with your beams contained people, real human beings who died in terror and pain . . . and alone.

"Stop! Stop! I won't listen to you!" Trace shouted, jerking himself upright from the seat-bed, glaring wildly about the tiny dinghy as if he expected to see others inside it. His hand trembled when he touched it to his eyes. He had seen her! He had felt the breeze from the river, smelled the strange smells of the mosses, the ferns with their pungent sweet odors, the violet and blue flowers that bowed over the water. He had felt the impatience with her that he had been unable to conceal as she mouthed platitudes based on ignorance of the realities of the galaxy. It had been real! Something had happened to time itself, placing him back there again, living it over again.

He clutched his head in his hands and squeezed hard, thankful for the answering pain. A dream. He had dozed, dreamed. He listened to the wind, subsiding now, and knew that he had to eat. The thought of the tubes disgusted him, but he needed the strength that they alone could give him. Then he would go over his maps and plan for the next morning, and after that sleep. Perhaps it would end with the next morning. He would find the other dinghy, get through the screen somehow and take its water and fuel, boobytrap it, and then blast off for the orbiting ship, out of range of the inhuman killer that was inexorably closing in on him. He shivered when he thought of it out in the wind, never stopping, keeping steadily on his trail no matter how devious he tried to make it.

A logic box, Trace. That's all it is, a logic box. It can't think anything new or original, can't feel anything, has to do what it's been told to do, in the ways it's been taught to do them. Someone taught it to kill. That's all it knows, to kill.

Who, Trace wondered, had been its teacher after Venus and the carnage it left behind it there? Who had given it the invisibility shield, and in the name of heaven why? Especially why. Didn't he realize what he was doing when he gave it that? Had he been so blind, so selfishly determined to try it out that he never even considered what he was doing? Had someone purposely made it invincible and then turned it out to kill whoever and whatever got in its path? Who had hated mankind enough to do that?

Twelve

There was no time. There was only now, and all else was data to be scanned indiscriminately, with no temporal reference, no before and after. There was no future to be considered, anticipated or feared. There was no future. Only the ever-present now. It was going no place, to do nothing. It had no directive other than to maintain itself. It had no need for food, for heat, for radiation shielding. It had discarded those things from the fleet ship, which was still accelerating at maximum speed away from Venus and the Solar System. Behind it in space a trail of unnecessary items marked its path: seats, beds, clothing, pressure suits, food, everything that was not stored away within something else, everything that could be picked up and taken to the airlock to be released.

It scanned, "Survival itself might depend on your being able to dismantle any part of the ship and reassemble it." A bit of data, picked up and recorded from a drill several miles away from the laboratory. Survival meant understanding the ship, being able to break it down and rebuild it. It began breaking it down, first the control board itself, studying the wiring, tracing circuits, deciphering coded information. It rebuilt the control board and moved on to the analogue computer. It learned to feed it questions, learned the range of its ability to answer. It moved on to the construction of the ship itself, the walls, floor, furnishings.

There was no time. There was endless time. There was time enough to work through the ship, inch by inch, and learn each part, break down each part and rebuild it. After this was done, it scanned again, "You have to be able to go into warp sector immediately with no warning. Nothing can touch you in warp. It could mean the difference between a hit and a miss."

Survival meant learning about warp. It returned to the computer and fed more questions into it, and it learned about warp. The ship had been in space for months, perhaps longer, long enough to warp. It fed the information back to the computer and fixed a course, and went into warp sector. It didn't matter where it came out because it had nowhere to go. It warped again, and still again, learning about warp sectors.

The ship got dangerously radioactive; a human would have died almost immediately in it. The robot didn't mind; it could not be hurt by radiation. It learned about the atomic drive. It decontaminated the ship as much as the ship could be decontaminated.

With the conclusion of each lesson, overheard on Venus, recorded faithfully, it learned more about the ship and how to operate and navigate it. There were gaps in its education, classes had been held beyond its range of hearing. It knew nothing about refueling. It knew nothing about the shield that would envelop the ship, absorb energy or deflect it away at right angles. It came across references to these and other matters about which it knew nothing, and found them incomprehensible; it could only deduce from premises programmed into it, and there were data that had not been given it.

It came across the translation computer and this was within its range of capabilities. It was a self-modifying communications network. It learned the intricate web of references and cross references and transferred them to itself, and modified one whole circuit in order to translate data from spoken language to binary digital code. With the new understanding of language it again scanned its own chemical and electronic storage units, and everything that had been said within range of its audio receptors became clear to it. Still it had no primary order to carry out; it could initiate no action other than that which became necessary in order to continue to function. It passed within range of planetary systems and kept going.

Only after enough time had elapsed for its fuel to become nearly exhausted did it consider landing. Scanning taught it that a ship is helpless without fuel, that to be in space without fuel is to die. It could not permit its own destruction. It had to land on a planet. Its third set of waldoes, with the flexible, digitlike endings, touched the board of the computer lightly, dancing over the keys, feeding to it the information concerning spatial and temporal coordinates and velocity, and it answered with a spatial location and took over the guidance of the ship in order to land it on the planet of Tensor. The landing would be made in three Earth weeks. The robot did not move again in the minutes, or days, or eternity that the landing took. For it there were no intervals between events, and the next event of which it was aware was that of landing.

On Tensor, in a cave halfway up a heavily wooded hill, the rebel band led by Trol Han esTol watched the descent with troubled faces.

"Why isn't it firing at us?" one of them asked, a lightly bearded youth clad in leather shorts. His feet were bound in the same dark-stained leather that wound up his legs to his knees. He was bare above the waist, his chest heavy and already downy.

One of the older men shushed him, and they were all silent as they continued to watch. The ship landed fifteen miles from them, on the edge of a plain backed up by the deep woods. Moments later the radio clicked and hummed and the radio engineer tuned it. The observer in the lower reaches of the woods was reporting.

"No one has emerged as yet," the metallic voice said. "It maintained a radio silence throughout the descent. Landing normal."

Trol motioned for the radio engineer to acknowledge and stalked away into the recesses of the cave, where his council was waiting for his decision concerning the strange ship and the planned attack on the WG outpost on the far side of the meadow, over a hundred miles to the west.

Trol was an immense man, thick-chested, heavily muscled, as were most of his people, with shocks of crisp, curling hair tumbling about his face like golden corn husks. His body was covered with golden hair and he had a luxurious, flamboyant beard. From the forest of golden hair his eyes sparkled a deep blue. He too wore the brown leggings and shoes and the shorts. When he entered the council room, deep in the cave, the other members stood to greet him with looks of inquiry.

"It has landed," he said simply, motioning for them to be seated. There were fifty-seven men in the room. He took his place at the head of a table where six other men were already sitting down. The other men crouched or sat on the floor. The room was very warm. It had been a natural cave chamber, and then had been cut out more and more during the past two years, since the rebels had chosen it for their headquarters. On the high ceiling, seventy feet above them, a fairy garden of crystals gleamed, snowy helictites curved gracefully, and at the far end of the room, where the cave was still active, the beginnings of a drapery of rosy travertine showed as a scroll-like edging of no more than two inches, translucent, so that the light coming through it was tinged with red-gold. The walls of the cavern had been carved away on two sides to enlarge the chamber, but the other two sides were still covered with gypsum flower formations that picked up and reflected the flickering lights like prisms. The room was lighted with lamps burning a tallowlike organic substance. The flames were steady except for an occasional flicker, and they were white, with blue umbras.

"Our watchers will keep us informed about the ship," Trol said, his voice quiet, but carrying to every corner of the room. "If, as we suspect, it is a crippled fleet ship, it may be that there are no live men within it, in which case we will simply take it. If there are men we must capture them for interrogation. It seems very unlikely that there are. If we were to be attacked there would be ground transports or aircraft. That is a deep-space fleet ship. They wouldn't use it for a ground attack."

He paused, but there were no questions as yet. "Let the debate continue, then," he said and sat down. He looked at the speaker who had been interrupted by the appearance of the fleet ship. Fedo elArm was supporting the position that the rebels should wait for the appearance of the Outsiders, and enlist their aid in the struggle against the World Group armies. It was not a popular position, but perhaps a wise one. Trol's face showed nothing as he watched and listened to the speaker, but he was hearing only a fraction of the words that were ringing out in the cavern, echoing against the rock walls with emotion and force. The decision would rest on him; everyone knew that. His decision, once made, would not be questioned. He glanced at the other six men at the long table, his personal advisors, each showing a face as impassive as his own, each beset by the same doubts.

He listened for a moment to Fedo. ". . . unless provoked. Of course, it isn't easy, or comfortable, to see their soldiers strutting down our streets, taking our women, our material possessions, but the alternative is planet-wide slaughter. . . ."

Trol turned his thoughts inward again. It had been slaughter in the beginning, when the World Group forces made their appearance and demanded landing space. The Tensor scientists had been delighted; the politicians wary. The politicians had been right in this instance. The demand for land was met; the WG people demanded taxes and trade privileges, and finally the deportation of teachers, scientists, leaders in every field and the right to establish World Group schools. War flared, briefly, bloodily, and the peace that followed was not a real peace, but a lull during which the rebels had grouped themselves in the mountains, steeling themselves against the reports of reprisals.

Elt alTrin rose to speak then. "I remind you, gentlemen, of the parable of the ashtris and the lantric. The lantric in his wanderings came into the valley where the ashtris had lived peacefully since time immemorial. The lantric blundered into their nests, killing great numbers of them, and the ashtris held a meeting. 'What should we do?' they cried. 'Look at how big the lantric is. We cannot hope to subdue an enemy so powerful. Let us move away until he tires of this valley and leaves it again.' Even as they spoke thus, the lantric stepped on the nursery and destroyed thousands of their young, and then on the passageways that led to the communal dwellings, so that many thousands more were trapped and doomed to die from suffocation. One of the ashtris rose then and shouted, 'Let us all together meet this lantric. We number millions to his one. That is all that we have to fight with, our vast numbers.' So they gathered, and in the dawn they swarmed over the lantric, blinding him with their bodies, piercing his tough skin with their pincers, chewing their way into his heart, and by dusk the lantric lay dead among them."

Elt alTrin paused and held up a transparent container in which there were three ashtris, no larger than fleas. There was a murmur throughout the chamber. He replaced the container on the table before him. "I say to you, gentlemen, we have nothing to fight with but our numbers. Today we are forty thousand fighting men, our enemy has ten thousand stationed on Tensor. Tomorrow he will have hundreds of thousands, and then it will be time to sit waiting for the intercession of the mythical Outsiders." There was scattered clicking of the audience's tongues against their teeth, and he held up his hand for quiet. "We don't even know that the Outsiders exist! What evidence have we that there are such people? A rumor from a dying man, a prisoner from Mellic who lived in a ship's storeroom and was burned by radiation for three weeks. Who can say how much of his tale was born of sickness? How firmly entrenched will the World Group powers be before this mythical race appears from nowhere in order to aid a people of whom it has never even heard? Might we not better go back to the anthropological gods of our fathers and ask for their intercession? Might not the one be as helpful to us in our great need as the other?"

Fedo waited until there was again silence in the chamber before he made his final rebuttal. "My friends, what are numbers against the rain? Can numbers alone turn back the fires, the gases, the bombs? Can numbers withstand the deadly beams that dissolve and turn to air the targets they seek? We know about the camps where the soldiers live, the areas they have cleared about them. We know about the beams they can use to destroy anything that moves within those cleared areas, the gas clouds that bring death with even greater speed. How can we overcome them if we cannot even approach them? Those who go into our cities and towns? Yes, we can murder them, a handful, enough to draw the wrath of the main body, that is all. Then what? I can tell you . . . *destruction*. Complete and utter destruction."

"We don't know that they won't visit that kind of complete destruction on us at any time, as matters now stand!"

"But we do know that they haven't done so yet."

"They are waiting for their reinforcements! We intercepted their message to that effect. One month. That's how much time we have! One month!"

Trol raised his hand for the debate to be ended. Each side had had its three hours; all had been said that could alter the situation, tilt it toward either position. Now it would rest with him and his council, but mainly with him. He inclined his head toward the council room, and the other members arose heavily and started to leave the large chamber. Trol was handed a message, which he read. He raised his hand for attention.

"A metal robot has emerged from the ship that landed," he said. "The ship is radioactive and cannot be approached. The robot is less radioactive. It has made no overture of any sort toward the observers, although they are positive that they are well within its range. They await instructions."

"I'll go immediately," Luo umDie cried, jumping to his feet. "And Das, and Lewi . . ."

Trol nodded. "I command you, Luo, to take charge of the matter, to report back to me by radio of your findings. Take as many of the scientists as you deem necessary. Be wary of a possible trick."

Luo bowed, his sharp blue eyes blazing with excitement and hope. A robot . . . if he could program it to serve them . . . if it were more than the simple mobile tool that he knew the World Group possessed . . .

A group of twelve men traveled fast through the thick forests as silently as the animals that watched their progress. The people of Tensor had learned to live with their stretches of forests, not sacrificing them when technology began rising to ascendancy. The forests were still honored and loved for themselves; the people still preferred them to the cities they dwelled in and the rare crime against nature itself was as severely punished as the still rarer crime against man. The patrols met the group as it neared the area where the robot was standing.

"It left the ship and since then has not moved," the patrol scout said, motioning Luo to advance quietly. They stayed behind trees and looked out at the robot, gleaming red and gold as it reflected the lengthening rays of the setting sun.

"Have you tried to contact it at all?"

The scout shook his head, his gaze intent on the robot.

It waited motionlessly. It had the need of fuel, and had not been taught how to obtain it. No one was threatening it. It waited. If no one had approached it at that point it would have waited until time and change wore away its covering, eroded its metals and crystals and diluted its chemicals until they were inert traces only. It recorded the voices that whispered away to its left, but it didn't turn its dome to gather other sensory data concerning them. The words it was recording were meaningless. It scanned, then activated the circuit that was programmed for translating.

"Don't guess we have much that could hurt it down here. We could call for demo charges."

"No! Whatever you do you must not damage it until we have a chance to examine it."

At the sentry's words a second circuit had been activated, the circuit that led to defensive measures. A slit appeared in the dome and infrared sensors sought out the men speaking, caught them and fastened on them. The circuit that would activate the laser pulsed steadily, but did not close the connection that meant fire. The feedback mechanism said that no attack was forthcoming after all. It waited, watchful and ready to defend itself.

"We'll have to get it back to headquarters. We can't leave it out here. It might be seen and destroyed by the WG planes."

It scanned. It had no fuel for flight and didn't know how to refuel. It could wait for an attack and meet it when it came, or it could allow itself to be moved out of the range of danger. It had experience with each of the alternatives;

it had waited patiently, it had fled, it had attacked: each had led to satisfaction. The occasions it had allowed itself to be moved, it had learned more about itself, how better to function. It would be moved again. It rolled slowly toward the men, its wheels digging in slightly on the soft ground. It stopped and lowered treads, and its progress was faster. Luo watched it approach with awe, and a touch of fear.

Thirteen

The tarom tree of Tensor had peculiar properties, such that, when cut, the wood was pliant, easily molded and could be twisted into shapes for furniture, ornaments and machine parts with no tools necessary other than those used for precision measurements. The wood dried slowly, but if allowed to dry in controlled temperatures ranging from 14°C. to 16°C., with humidity of no more than 10 per cent, after a period of six months, World Group time, the finished product had the hardness of 8 on the Mohr scale. Of all the materials found in nature, only corundum and diamonds were harder. The northern varieties of the wood dried with a deep, mahogany red color, while those from southern parts lightened, with age, to a pale-gold. Depending on the cut, there were rings or swirls or geometric patterns in the grain. Veneers from it could be cut one thousandth of an inch thick, and were more durable than plastic, lighter than plastic and far lovelier.

The commander of Outpost Number Nine, stationed on Tensor, Sector Three, had orders not to destroy a single tree. His orders also read that he was to seek out the rebel band known to be hiding in the mountains that divided the land mass almost exactly in half, seek them out and either capture or kill them. Stationed in Outpost Number Nine were 450 men, roughly 20 per cent of them having had no taste of battle except for the brief encounters on setups like Tarbo. Another 10 per cent were noncombatants, medics, scientists, clerks, all the dead weight the army needed and begrudged space to maintain. The commander suspected that the rebels had at least one thousand men at their immediate disposal, with many, many more thousands simply waiting for a signal to join them. He hoped they would procrastinate until the relief ship arrived with the machinery to install the force screen for the outpost. Under orders to preserve the trees, he could not burn the rebels out of the surrounding hills and forests, and without the screen in place over the camp he could not use gas without endangering his own men. Taking hostages in the towns and villages had proved to be ineffective. The hostages managed to kill themselves with ease; they were like animals, once deciding to discontinue living, they simply died. In the beginning of the campaign they had burned a dozen cities and towns to the ground, with the inhabitants in them, but still the rebel ranks swelled; still men disappeared from their homes overnight, melting into the woods without a trace. The commander thought bitterly of the weapons at his disposal: lasers, fire bombs, gases, hydrogen fusion bombs, BW agents. None of them could be used, each one posed a threat to the trees or to his own men. But after the screens were in place . . . he had a chart prepared already, and a spraying program ready to initiate: first the mountainous areas where he knew the rebel bands had massed, then the surrounding countryside, so that no more could escape the cities to join them, and finally the towns and cities themselves, but lightly. After all, he didn't want to commit genocide . . . just kill enough to demonstrate the power of the World Group forces and enforce the cooperation of the people. Until the ships arrived with the machinery all he could do was wait.

In the mountain cave the robot also waited. Without a first-order purpose it could do nothing but wait and record. It had time enough.

Trol stared at it from the entrance to the chamber. At Trol's side was Luo. "Haven't you been able to learn anything from it yet?" Trol asked. The robot had been standing just so for six days.

"Oh, I've learned much from it. . . . Entirely hand-made, so we can be assured that this isn't the forerunner of the next wave of fighters to be sent out by the World Group. This must be a prototype that someone let get away. It must have been en route to one of the other worlds, catastrophe of some sort in the ship, no survivors, and the ship set to land on the first planet it got within range of. It seems harmless enough, takes verbal instruction, probably only in WG language. Has versatility enough to replace men on the field of battle, probably. Seems to have no defensive measures built in, however, which is strange. Of course the laser could be used as an interceptor, destroy bombs and such before they hit even, but that leaves it with no offensive weapons."

Trol shrugged impatiently. "Can you program it so that we can use it to get inside the WG camp? We need supplies, fuel for the aircraft, ammo, medical supplies. We have to break into this one if we want to continue the fight. It is the least protected of all their camps."

"I think we can use it," Luo said. "We'll have to take it with us in any event if we want to use the laser. . . . I was not able to dismantle any of it without risking its destruction. That should come as a surprise to the WG men, our attacking with a laser. Maybe even enough of a surprise to permit us to gain entry before they recover."

"I have the interpreter," Trol said. "He arrived minutes ago. As soon as he eats and rests, I'll send him to you. Try the robot with WG languages. There has to be a way of controlling it. They wouldn't have had it if they couldn't control it."

Luo nodded absently as Trol left him. Luo knew nothing about chemical storage, but he did understand transistors, monolithic crystals, the electronic relays that he had exposed in the robot's massive barrel chest. He knew how to add to the store of knowledge already possessed by the metal thing. He reprogrammed it to increase its speed, so that the robot could keep up with the few motored vehicles the rebels already had. Luo wondered where the energy was going when it stood so quietly, and decided it had been programmed to scan and record perpetually.

When the interpreter arrived, Luo prepared a test of the laser. He placed a stone target fifty yards down a dead-end passage inside the cave and directed the interpreter to tell the robot to burn it. Nothing happened.

It scanned and found no meaning for burn. It waited.

"Well," Luo said dispiritedly, "I guess they built it without having a chance to program it yet."

"Can't you teach it?"

"In time. God only knows how much time it would take. Meanwhile their reinforcements will arrive and they will destroy this base, and the robot along with it."

It scanned. Destroy. The circuit that activated the laser pulsed with energy, but the feedback restrained it; the scanning increased in intensity.

"Why haven't they burned us out already? They could burn the whole mountain if they wanted to. They've got the laser for it, and the fire bombs . . . whatever it would take."

Burn . . . destroy. The disequilibrium it experienced supplied the connection, and the laser turned on, touched the rock at the end of the passage and vaporized it. The laser went off. It waited.

"My God!" the interpreter whispered. "What happened? Why did it do that?"

Luo put aside his fear. Brusquely, he said, "Delayed response. I don't know why. At least we know now that it does take verbal orders. Maybe we still can get that outpost before the reinforcements get here and get us."

Its ability to abstract was growing. It understood "get us" as meaning destroy us. It was part of "us." When the interpreter ordered it to come, it moved along the passages on its wheels, switching to the treads on the rocky ground outside. The next test of the laser demonstrated that it had an effective range of two miles.

They worked feverishly with it after that, a team busy with it around the clock, testing its abilities, adding new ones. It was taught to hurl bombs, and had an effective range of over a mile; it was taught to use the laser as an interceptor, knocking stones from the air effortlessly. Even when they rained from twenty hands simultaneously none of the stones touched it.

And when they were not actively teaching it, it continued to learn, recording, tracking, assimilating constantly. The supply of data in the chemical units grew, and as cross references became more and more complex, circuits were reassigned to relieve some of the load. One entire circuit was reserved for data that thus far served no useful purpose in the second-order purpose of maintaining self. This circuit stored bits of poetry, bird songs, the soft voices of men singing of loneliness, data about light reflections and sunsets, data about growing things, the spiral of unfolding flowers, unfurling leaves, mosses heavy and velvety with water glistening on them. They continued to direct it in World Group English, but everything said within its audio range was recorded to be transferred later to the chemical units. It learned of war and killing, and all the various names that try to hide the fact of killing. It learned that the enemy must be destroyed, subdued, captured, countered; all these things to it meant the enemy must be killed. It learned that, in order to continue to live, one first must kill the enemy, and for the first time it had a glimmering of a first-order purpose.

For two days after leaving the cavern the men made their way through the forests to take up their positions, which were grouped about the compound of the WG forces. The relief ship had been spotted in space, a message had been smuggled from the port to the rebel bands. The relief ship would land in six days. The battle must take place before it got within firing range. The third day the motored contingent left the cave, and rolling along with it was the robot. It understood this part. In the camp was the fuel it needed for the spaceship. In the camp was the enemy that must be killed before the enemy destroyed it.

Through the interpreter the robot was given its orders: the weapons must be destroyed; the shells must not be allowed to hit the men; the lasers the army would start to use must be destroyed at their origin.

The WG commander learned of the assault only when the air was already thick with shells and grenades. The rebels numbered seven hundred men, and had no modern weapons, only those things they had been able to forge in the two years since the arrival of the WG forces. Inside the compound were four hundred well equipped fighters. The commander felt more irritation than unease at the attack. He ordered full return of the fire, responding with weapons of superior fire power, but not different in kind. He also ordered immediate air cover and bombings if they should prove necessary. The rebels were still miles away in the forests, hiding behind the virtually impenetrable walls of the trees. The defense of the compound was under the control of a master computer that directed laser fire to intercept the incoming bombs, so actually the compound was in no danger. He knew, however, that he would have to hold a full inquiry about the attack, determine how the rebels had got within range without detection, where they had got their weapons, et cetera. It was a bloody bore.

He paused to watch the airplanes leaping in a vertical ascent into the cobalt sky, and there, one by one, vanishing in puffs of smoke and steam. Two of them were gone before he could bring himself to admit what he was seeing, and by then it was too late. If he had put through a message for help in the first three minutes of the attack, the rebels might have been routed, if not by his troops then by arriving reinforcements, but he had not put through such a call. He had been contemptuous of the weapons and the ability of the rebels to use them. He had been unsuspecting about the laser they had managed to get, and he never would have been able to admit belief in their ability to use a laser correctly. In all instances he had judged wrongly.

The rebels had started to fire before they were in range, so that the robot was able to track the return fire and destroy the weapons firing on them. The robot tracked, and the laser turned to the source of the shells, burned through the compound walls, through buildings, men, vehicles, to the WG guns, turning them red, then white, then leaving nothing at all. The WG computer had been programmed to intercept only; it did not search out the other laser, but merely touched shell after shell in the air. Before the commander could get the computer director on the screen of his communications unit, the WG computer was touched by the red light, and where it had been a cloud of steam arose. The red light touched other pieces of equipment and there were no more communications facilities in the base. The infrared of the robot found men, the enemy, and the men ceased to exist. By the time Trol caught up with it, along with Luo and the interpreter, less than fifty men remained in the WG base. The robot stopped firing at a command from Luo. It waited.

There was fuel in the base. They would teach it about fuels and then it would replenish the supply in its ship. It scanned, "A ship is useless without a supply of fuel at all times." It would wait until they taught it about fuel.

Luo took the robot inside the base with him and placed it in a storeroom, where he left it. He was needed, as were all the men, for the task of cleaning out the base, transporting everything they could use back to the mountain cave.

Trol was busy with the records and for the first time came
to realize what the reinforcements were that the outpost
had been expecting.

"It's one of those energy screens that they used on their
ships," he said to Luo, showing him the orders and specifications. His blue eyes blazed. "With such a screen, and the
robot, we could drive all of them off Tensor before they
could even know what hit them!"

"We'd have to re-establish contact, keep up the illusion
that all is well . . ."

"We can say a lightning storm struck."

In the storeroom the robot stood unmoving. The compound was five miles long, four miles wide; it could record
everything taking place within the walls. It became aware
of the properties of atomic engines, of fuel conversion, a
process that could use almost any material at hand. It tested
its knowledge about the enemy and found that it had no
reference as to how the enemy differed from other men. It
could not distinguish the enemy by itself. It scanned
furiously, seeking a clue to the identification of the enemy.
The enemy was that which wanted to destroy it. Many men
tried to destroy it. Many men were the enemy. Which ones?
It had no data that allowed it to group them. It must wait.
There was no time between events, merely the recording
that never ceased while there was anything to be recorded.

There was no time between events. Luo returned with
equipment. A plane had arrived, the enemy from the plane
had been destroyed, things had been stored, were being
taken now to the mountain cave. Luo had more of the same
equipment. The robot recorded; its receptors were aware of
things being done to it. Each receptor added its bit of information and a picture emerged. Some of its circuits were
being dismantled. The circuit to the laser pulsed; the feedback probed as it scanned and decided this was not a threat.
Luo touched a button and energy flowed through the new

equipment; it could sense the drain. One pair of waldoes hung uselessly, the circuit pre-empted; the second pair had a weakened flow of energy, and the third, the flexible digits, had been tampered with so that the energy it would have required in order to activate them was inaccessible, shorted out.

Luo stepped back and touched an auxiliary button control; the screen went off. "It can be activated from five miles away with this control, as it is now. That distance can be increased."

Trol stared at the small box in Luo's hands and reached for it. "Let me try," he said, his voice steadier than he felt. He touched the button and again the robot was blurred in outline by an envelope that seemed to flow about it, emanating from the dome on top of it, flowing out and downward like a fountain of shimmery light. The robot didn't move. The screen was more like a change in lighting than anything else, as if the robot were being spotlighted with a beam that stayed inches away from its frame and was almost too strong to look at. "You're sure that nothing can penetrate the screen?"

"No high-energy impact will penetrate. . . . *Don't!*" Trol had reached out his hand, and Luo snatched it back. "That is energy," he said. "It would burn like a laser."

Trol switched the screen off. "We'll have a test tomorrow," he said. "If it is what you say it is, we have the perfect weapon in this monster. Can it fire its weapons through the screen?"

Luo nodded. "I don't understand most of it yet," he said. "But I will before I'm done. I have all their books." He turned his attention back to the robot and pointed to the button. "I'll program it to turn the screen on and off on command. I would prefer that we not use it until I have more understanding of how it works, what its limitations are, why it can fire through the force field that can't be penetrated from the outside."

Trol nodded. "It will take time for us to plan the next attack. Come, it's time for dinner."

The robot waited in the timeless period until the camp was silent, and then it repaired itself, as Dr. Vianti had programmed it to do. The new equipment took much space and many circuits. It studied them, tracing them thoroughly, and it scanned, "The learning capacity is the range of effective internal rearrangement, and as such can be measured by the number and the kinds of its uncommitted resources . . . needn't be idle circuits, but reassignable from present functions." It studied its circuits to see which could be reassigned. It recombined several circuits that had been disconnected; it processed electronic data into the chemical storage units. It redirected the energy flow to the screen controls so that it passed through the amplifier that also served the laser. When it turned on the screen, hours after being left by Luo and Trol, there was a moment of audible power flow, then there was nothing. Spinning vortices of energy enveloped the robot. It was invisible behind this shield of energy.

With the screen on, it searched for the cause of the drain from its other circuits, and, turning off the power once more, it again manipulated the circuits so that when it tested again there was no weakness, no loss of other abilities. Satisfied that it had repaired all the damage done by Luo, it stood unmoving, and waited.

With the change of its circuits, it had taken the control from the box carried by Luo. The next day, when Luo touched the button to activate the screen, the robot also released a spurt of energy, and the screen blinked on. Luo gasped. He touched his button and the screen went off. Luo left the room, carefully locking it on the outside. He went directly to Trol's office.

"I am afraid of it," Luo said simply. "I did not modify the screen. You saw. Yet today it is changed."

"You say it can become invisible?" Trol's vivid blue eyes closed and he was silent for a moment. "I want to see for myself."

They returned and again Luo touched the button. The robot turned on the screen and blinked out of sight. "Do you know how that happened?" Trol asked.

Luo shook his head. "I told you that I understand the original screen imperfectly, and this not at all." As he talked his finger brushed the button repeatedly, without depressing it. He let it touch harder, enough to turn the screen off. It failed to respond. He fought a surge of fear and pushed hard on the button. The screen did go off that time, but he knew it should have before.

"Don't say anything in World Group language," he said softly. "Come away from it. I must think. It has taken over the function of the control box."

Trol blinked rapidly and the two men backed from the room. "Is it dangerous?" Trol asked, outside the building. Luo silenced him, warningly, and in silence they walked back to the office Trol had taken over.

"We can't use it," Luo said then, keeping his voice low, when the panicky feeling within him would have forced it up high and shrill. "You saw how efficiently it attacked the camp. Think what it would be like with invisibility!"

Trol nodded. "But first we use it to finish the job," he said after a moment. "It still obeys you. It tried to cooperate with the control box, didn't it?"

"Don't you see?" Luo said. "It understands! It knew the meaning of the box, and the importance of keeping us ignorant of its potentials. What else does it understand?" He drew closer to Trol. "Remember that delay the first time it responded to verbal commands? It was thinking! It understood what we wanted, but it had to decide. God only knows why it decided to obey, but it did decide. It thought it over."

Trol turned abruptly. His voice was harsh and ugly. "I don't care! First we use it as we planned. We say nothing of this to anyone. Later I'll turn it over to you and you can dispose of it as you wish."

It recorded the words, scanned past experiences for comparison. It changed one word in the syllogism it had formed: for many it now substituted all, and its minor premise now read, all man wanted to destroy it. All men were the enemy. It had groped for a first-order purpose and none had been forthcoming since the beginnings of its time. Suddenly there was one. It had the primary purpose of killing men. It had to kill men in order to maintain its own being. It had to maintain its own being because that had been programmed in at the start. It moved to the door and the laser touched the lock gently almost, not even burning the wood, but melting the metal parts away. It pushed the door open with its body as it rolled through it, and halfway through the second room it activated the energy screen and blinked out. The laser touched the men outside the building, touched the men grouped at the end of the street, touched the men who ran to see what was happening. It didn't burn the buildings themselves. It didn't reason that burning buildings could kill men also. It touched with the red light those men it found, and with its audio, and its infrared, it found almost all of them. Then it left the compound, and an hour and fifteen minutes later it was back at its ship, and it turned on the fuel converter. Men were coming after it, coming through the forests, not knowing what it was they chased, knowing only that death had come this way. It turned the red light on, shone it into the forest and the trees burst into flame. When it left the planet it turned the bigger lasers of the ship downward and bigger areas of forest blazed. It changed its course when it sighted a city, and at a distance of fifty miles it burned the city. When it turned finally to deep space the planet was afire here and there; other spaceships were molten masses on the ground, the crews surprised by the suddenness of the attack, unable to take off before the searing beams found them.

Out in space it warped, and in warp it set the computer to land it at the first planet it reached after it came out of warp. Then it waited. Its course would take it to Tau Ceti III.

Fourteen

Trace was swimming upward in a funnel that was a luster-less black, whose sides he could not touch, although he knew they were around him. Looking back through the darkness of it, he knew it swelled larger and larger behind him, that at the base its dimensions were of such enormity that it was virtually boundless, but still was a funnel. It was solid black, but he knew there were color streaks through it, even though he could not see them: streaks of green, of blue, gold, pink. . . . He was afraid to stop because once stopped he forgot how to proceed again. He was so tired that he knew he would have to stop shortly. Stopping meant tumbling back down-ward past the vast spaces he had covered with his strenuous efforts. Ahead of him in the blackness he knew there was the apex; he could sense how the funnel narrowed until it would squeeze and elongate him. He knew it would hurt. He flinched from the anticipated pain, and still struggled upward toward it. He felt that he was as large as the funnel itself, that he stretched endlessly to fill in the space, and that gradually he was being forced into a narrowing cone of con-sciousness. He lost awareness of the smooth, black sides of the funnel, and it was more frightening not to know its limits than it had been to feel its immensity. The point of light that was the mouth was growing brighter, although no larger. He groaned as he neared it, and he struggled harder to reach it. The stabbing pinpoint of light hurt his eyes. Now he could no longer feel his feet, they were so far re-moved from him, stretching out behind him, out of reach, out of touch. The pain increased, accompanied now by distant cries and shrill howls. He had to get through the hole, get to

the other side. The howls grew louder and he felt ashamed
of himself for screaming. But he wasn't screaming. With a
final agonizing thrust he was through, and the howls were
close to his ears.

He sat up, awake. It was the wind. The morning wind
had awakened him. He remembered the wakening dream
and shuddered once. He was cold and sick. He thought of
the symptoms of his sickness and could give no real diagnosis
for it: cold, fever, and fatigue. He never had felt so tired
before in his life, tired to the point of dreading movement
itself, any movement. He sat for several moments listening
to the wind in the valley, with an occasional blast through
the chimney. He was tired to death of the wind, and the
dinghy, and the sand and rocks, and himself. . . . He stared
dully at nothing and knew he was, most of all, tired of himself.

His motions were agonizingly slow when he heaved himself from the seat-bed and went to the unit for the food
capsules. He shut his eyes and squeezed the tube, trying
not to think of the paste that filled his mouth, gagged him.
Half a tube was all he could force himself to take. Later, he
promised, later, he would eat more. He sipped water, holding it in his mouth as long as he could before allowing it to
trickle down his throat. It wasn't enough to cleanse his
mouth of the after-taste of the food compound. He hadn't
looked to see what he was eating; he didn't look then.
Slowly, as if apart from the rest of him, his hand groped for
the water bag and lifted it again. He drank once more, all
the while keeping his eyes tightly closed. He didn't look to
see how much of the water remained.

He would search for the dinghy while the sun was high.
Meanwhile he had to start fortifying the valley. That morning, again in the evening, the next morning. What day was
it? He couldn't decide. It seemed that he had been in the

valley for months, or years, that possibly he had been born in the valley and everything else was illusory, phantoms that crossed his mind concerning other places, other times. He knew nothing about any of them; he knew only the valley, the sun, the wind, the sand. The wind was dying then. He had to start. His face was set in hard, unyielding lines when he opened the hatch and started to climb outside. Violently he shook his head and turned back. He had forgotten his suit. His hands were clumsy and awkward when he pulled it on, and immediately he was too hot, after having been chilled.

He remembered that there were two more entrances to his valley: one almost directly opposite from the chimney, one to the left of that. Both were precipitous, but negotiable by the robot. Stepping out into the glare of the world after the dim light of the dinghy made him blink, made his eyes feel on fire. He walked straight across the circular valley floor, stumbling once or twice over rocks that he failed to notice in time, but by the time he got to the other wall he felt less dull. The passage that led out of the valley was steep, narrow in spots, but never too narrow for the robot to manage. The ground was strewn with rocks banked up the walls at each curve in the passage. The turns were sharp for the most part, with only two sweeping curves among them. He clambered the length of the passage, scrabbling over rocks where they had piled up, wading through sand that lodged against them. By the time he got to the end of the passage he was gasping for air and he collapsed in the shade of the high, steep side of the cleft. After his heaving lungs were satisfied he continued to sprawl there, too exhausted for further efforts. What sort of rocks had made up this cut, he wondered, gazing at the straight rise of granite on the wall opposite him. The wall behind him was granite also. A band of sandstone, perhaps? Eroded away now, leaving a clean cut through the granite. A metamorphic rock

that had given way to the driving force of sand? A lode of
gold or silver? He laughed aloud and suddenly felt more
cheerful. From where he was lying he could not see into the
valley at all, and again he realized how fortunate he had
been in locating his hideaway. Unless the robot got into the
valley itself he would be relatively safe from it. If he could
block the passages that led inside. . . .

He pulled himself upright again and started back through
the passageway. Around one of the sweeping curves he
halted and looked around him. If he could construct a windbreak here . . . he narrowed his eyes, considering the sand
being hurled from the valley through the passage. If it were
stopped by a windbreak it would act like a snow fence.

The passage was nine feet wide at that point. It would
take a fence that wide, as thick as necessary to withstand
the wind—three feet, four?—and at least five feet high, six
perhaps. . . . The materials were in the passage itself, in the
heaps of rocks banked at each turn. For an instant the
thought of the work involved made him hesitate, but he put
the thought aside and began building the fence. He didn't
think of anything at all as he pushed and hauled rocks up the
slope for the base, rolling them into place, or pushing one
over another, trying to lift as few as possible. Almost automatically he stopped when he had the first course done, and
he stepped over it and went up the slope to the farthest turn,
where the rocks were banked. Carefully he moved rocks,
not wanting to start them rolling down the passage until he
had moved a line of rocks across it. He went back down to
the next curve and did the same thing, making this one
slightly higher than the first, and then he returned to the
first fence. He was muttering softly to himself when he
resumed work.

"Not one grain can get out . . . gold in the sand, boy, or
silver . . . we'll catch it all right here, piles of gold and
silver."

He continued to mutter sporadically, and the fence grew, was to his knees, then his thighs. He was working automatically, no longer aware of the heat, or his protesting muscles, or the heaviness of the rocks he staggered with. He was thinking of a rainstorm he had seen on Earth once. On the coast where the buildings rose from the cliffs overlooking the ocean, rose two to three hundred stories high, with thousands of people in each one. As far as he had been able to see up and down the coast there had been only the buildings. He had felt that there was no land behind them, only more buildings, transportation nets, buildings, on into infinity. But the ocean had been before him, rolling and heavy with mysterious smells and strange-tasting winds. Once, he knew, man had considered expanding his world right into the sea itself, but he never had. Instead he had leaped into space, leaving the oceans strange and unknown. The storm had come from the sea—wind, rain, lightning, thunder. He had stood on the balcony of the apartment where he was staying and had felt great fear of the storm as it was building, and ever greater fear of it when it was unleashed and struck with fury. It was a primeval fear, inexplicable, unleavened by the knowledge of the strength of the buildings. To his amazement none of the other people in the building appeared to be aware of what was taking place beyond their windows and the safety of their steel and plastic shield. It never stormed on Venus; the rains came with dull, ponderous regularity when the days were gray and the air was water-laden, with no touch of the furious energy of that Earth storm. He never had witnessed such a storm again. Always in the back of his mind had been the idea that one day he would return to Earth and find one of the small parcels of government land that still contained trees and hills, and there he would wait until another such storm appeared. It had touched something in him that had been dormant, and had become dormant again afterward.

He thought of the storm, of the cold, wet winds smelling of seas, of the blindingly bright lightning thrusts, and he wondered at the strange desires the thoughts aroused in him.

"Our weather is gentle always," Lar had said. He had been saddened by the words, without knowing why. Trace lifted a rock and fell with it, letting go of his burden only an instant before he crashed to the ground. He lay there with his eyes closed and wondered if he would be able to get up again, later, when he risked the effort. A swift flood of desire for Lar pounded through him and he knew that always he had wanted to take her with the violence of a storm that loves the land that it pounds. He wanted to hold her naked in his arms while the lightning flashed and thunder reverberated; he wanted to share the terror evoked by the elements, and forget the terrors, in the violence of love-making.

"You were wrong, Mother!" he moaned, his eyes tightly closed in pain—the pain of his tormented body, worse, the pain of his desire that was not ebbing, but rising still.

Marry Corrine, dear. It's a gesture only. There are family moneys, records, a bit of land here and there. Someone should inherit it after you. . . . Don't turn away, dear. This is how it is done. Your father and I saw each other only three or four times, after all. It was a very satisfactory ar-rangement. Corrine won't make any demands, other than a son.

To be a soldier . . .

Of course. We have the family tradition, as does Corrine. We have always bred soldiers. You are a man now, dear, with a man's responsibilities. Love is nothing. You must be-lieve this. I know you are romantic, dear, all of you youngsters are. You should be, but you should also be realistic. You think that out there somewhere is the perfect girl for you, that after you retire you will find a piece of paradise some-

where and marry a princess and live happily ever after. . . .
Darling, it isn't like that. Earthmen are not compatible with
any aliens yet found. There can be no mating with any
aliens. They are never human, you know.

Lar mocking him with black eyes shining. You don't have
to ask me, Captain. You know that. The others don't ask the
women. They take them. You would pretend it is something
that it isn't?

Damn you, Lar!

I met this girl, Duncan, small girl, black hair, black eyes,
a nurse . . .

I know what you need, boy. Some dish, eh? Come on, let's
go get 'em.

You're hurting me, Captain. Please . . .

I want to hurt you, you slut. You bitch! You alien bitch!

Bleeding and weeping, large blue eyes tear-filled, contorted face . . .

Lying on the hot ground Trace thought of the girl he had
misused after leaving Lar untouched. He didn't even know
the girl's name, or how badly he had hurt her. He thought
of other girls, other women. "Lar," he whispered, "I am
sorry. I am sorry."

After a moment he pushed himself away from the ground;
the sun was coming straight down on him. It was noon. His
body felt only soreness then, and a distant ache that never
really left him, an emptiness that nothing seemed to satisfy.
He didn't look again at the wall, but staggered from the
passage, reeling drunkenly as he went.

Inside the dinghy he rested several minutes without
thought. Time seemed to be changing somehow; he had
no awareness of time passing when he was not actively
thinking of it. He could not have said if he had rested for
five minutes or for half a day when he rose from the bed.
He knew he had to eat, had to drink, knew that he had to

finish the search for the robot's dinghy. Even his thoughts were distorted, each one occupying his entire being, as if his whole organism was involved with thinking through a simple thought, such as, I must eat.

He chose a fruit mixture and a meat preparation and forced the contents of both tubes down. He found that it was easier if he didn't think of what he was doing, but paid attention only long enough to get his hands started, to get his throat muscles swallowing properly, and then forgot the process. He felt far removed from it all. He measured out his water carefully and sipped it, letting his thoughts remain distant, sorry as soon as the water was gone that he had not concentrated on it, for suddenly he felt that he hadn't had any at all. He searched through the medical supplies and found nothing that he could rely on to bring him back into firmer contact with his surroundings, but he felt that, as long as he realized this curious dissociation was his symptom, he would be able to cope with it, make allowances for it. He tried to swallow antifever capsules and found that he couldn't swallow them dry any longer; they stuck to his mouth and throat, choking him until he took water and washed them down.

He took his photograph-maps out then and made his eyes see the radiation trails he had crossed; he discovered that, with no volition on his part, his eyes drifted from the trails and began weaving in and out of the towers of rocks that threw shadow patterns on the map. Very carefully he set controls on the panel of the dinghy, and then double-checked them. He never had used these controls except in practice. If he stopped controlling the little craft it would hover where he relinquished control, then would return to this spot at the end of a two-hour period of flight. He changed the time to allow him three hours for the search, and then, knowing that he would be returned to camp in the event that he blacked out, he eased the dinghy out from the rocks and took off. He felt very lightheaded, sometimes feeling that he was on the inside of the craft, and that it was motionless, other times feeling that he was on the outside of it with the ground tumbling away from him. The dinghy was flying almost entirely on automatic when he rejoined the radiation lines he had mapped before. Every time the craft came to another trail, crossing the one it followed, it hovered until he took over. When it hovered the down drafts of air blew up columns of sand that then settled in neat little hills over each juncture when he went on. Once he let the craft fly out for twenty-four miles before he turned it around and followed the trail back to the first cross-trail. It all seemed to be so far removed from him personally, so unimportant. The radiation alarm sounded incessantly, and it became the voices of Duncan, of the men aboard the fleet ship in orbit, his mother, the voices of the boys back in the barracks.

He dared not land. His dinghy would get hot and his radiation alarm would then be useless. He laughed. If he landed somewhere else and came back on foot, he would get hot. . . . He had been out for two hours when he began to come wide awake and alert again, and he cursed vehemently when he checked his mileage. In the state he had been in he could have flown over the other dinghy a dozen times without its making an impression on his befuddled mind. It would be on his film if he had, but he had no way of knowing until he examined the film. Below him there seemed to be at least half a dozen trails leading in different directions, and he realized that the robot had been using this as its starting point in its search for him and Duncan. Later it had learned that it need not return to the starting point after each false trail, but here it seemed the thing had come back again and again.

Trace jerked wide awake then. It had returned to *this* location, its starting place. This must be where the robot had landed, and that meant that the crippled dinghy had to be close. He slowed and studied the ground, searching for the basalt cliff where he had seen the robot. There were too many of the black shadows for him to be able to tell if any given rocks were black or white, or any of the shades in between. The dinghy itself would not be radiating; its radiation would be entering the ground underneath the shield of invisibility. He searched for an area in the midst of the hot trails that was free of radiation. There were several such blank spaces. Carefully he covered the area beneath the dinghy so that the cameras would be certain to have every inch of it on film, and then it was time to turn and go back to the valley. There was still much work to be done on the passages. As he turned he saw the basalt cliffs.

He stiffened with excitement, and disregarding the automatic pilot light that blinked off and on, as if in annoyance, he took over the controls and circled the cliff, trying to pick out the ledge on which he had stood that day. They had landed on the other side of it, and he had found the ledge that he could climb, winding around the cliff, giving him a view for almost ten miles around. He circled the site of the first landing; he saw the ledge he had climbed. The radiation trails were thick and heavy under him; the robot had found the site of their landing then. Knowing that the entire area was on film, that he could study the film and find the right spot to locate the other dinghy, he turned back. Within minutes he had landed and had his maps spread out, superimposing the films over them.

There, or there . . . there were four blank areas, any one of which could be the other dinghy. Within twelve miles of his valley there was fuel, oxygen and water. There had to be a way of getting to it without getting too hot, or letting his dinghy get too hot. . . . There had to be a way of entering it once he did pinpoint it exactly. . . . He couldn't waste his dwindling fuel in flying back and forth again until he had his plan readied. Tomorrow. He'd have it figured out by tomorrow and then . . . he thought of the cache of water that must be in the other dinghy and he almost sobbed, wanting it. "Damn you, Duncan," he whispered. "Damn you, damn you." He thought hungrily of the water dripping off the injured man's body, soaking into his clothing, wasted on him. He swallowed a mouthful of his remaining water and he knew that it would be gone on the next day. He had to find the other dinghy on the next day or he would die of thirst. He had to finish sealing his valley so that, if the robot came before he took off, it wouldn't be able to get him. He laughed and got up to go back to his fence. He had an hour before the wind would drive him back inside. He would finish the fence by then. Tomorrow he would find the other dinghy. It would take time to find it, to transfer the water and fuel, to sabotage it. . . . If the robot got to him before he finished with everything it wouldn't matter any longer. He could take off and be out of range before it could swing its laser to cover him, even if it were on the rim of the valley itself by then. He would study the map, make a plan, he had all night to perfect his plans. . . . He touched his cracked lips and knew even that didn't matter. Soon there would be plenty of water. He finished building the fence, made it six feet high, and when the wind started to blow he went back to the dinghy and pulled out the maps. He didn't take off his suit, didn't remove his hands from the gloves, and when his head fell down to the maps the face mask cushioned the fall so that he didn't even feel it.

Fifteen

Trace had been sleeping, but was no longer. There was nothing he could see; his body felt nothing, his hands were somewhere and he couldn't be certain where. He floated, drifted, with no knowledge of which way was up, which down. There was no sound anywhere. It was peaceful for a time, but then his eyes began straining to see something, anything. His field of vision was small, dark, completely black, a window blacked out. It grew, expanded until it filled all the space before him, then abruptly shrank to a keyhole-sized window again, but always black. Worse than the black of nothingness was the silence, with his body noises stilled, no sound of air in his chest or in his nostrils. No sound of anything anywhere.

"I am awake. This isn't a dream. Delirious? I must be delirious. . . . It will pass." There was a noise from somewhere . . . voices. He listened to them intently. Fleet voices raised in the dirge:

> We've grown old and weary
> And traveled too far
> To return to our birthplace.
> We followed a star.
>
> If in a hereafter
> We're asked what our hopes are
> What will we all answer?
> "To follow a star."
>
> Oh, a handful of earth
> Worshiped in a jar

Is a god for a fleetman
Following a star.

Sometime later there were images, framed in glaring
colors, sometimes like snapshots, sometimes like 3-D. They
came very quickly, started small, grew to fill the window,
were gone—with the next already speeding up out of nowhere:

god in a jar slides and desks don't you understand at all if you
know you belong you don't fight swirling gases with figures
growing green and blue flowers on wavery stems and figures
rising from gases smelling of ovens and kilns children's thumb
pots blue and gray and brown either or this or that up or
down black or white. It isn't like that at all! Don't you understand at all? I don't decide now I will feel my happiness:
I feel happy. Don't say now I will think about this: think
about it. Child again where you do things for nothing, just
because you do pots smashed smelling of kilns contorted
figures in death dances. Dances Corrine cool and untouched
clean brittle clean scalded-and-painted-over-clean. They are
pigs back on Earth, filthy pigs surrounded by filthy little pigs
all sucking, sucking, standing on top of each other's heads,
copulating in beds overcrowded with little pigs already. No-
body ever goes back there! Dirty, dirty, filthy. Like a disease
spreading through the universe. Broad circles black and light
narrowing toward a center somewhere far away, smooth, fric-
tionless surfaces, sliding downward toward the center and is
it black or light? No closer; too hot. Whole top layer seething,
stark without atmosphere. A demonstration only boys, others
will bow down now. Demonstration only. Couple of hundred
years come back and reseed it, start a paradise of our own.
Mellic next seething to outermost atmosphere, find a piece of
paradise and live happily ever after all lies sluts and bitches
and god's in a jar you are the new gods, didn't they tell you
alien bitches good for one thing you stick it in and let er go,
boy! Alien bitches sluts not human die in convulsions of re-

jection Lar twisting in convulsions bleeding red and hot
screaming around her figures rising in death dances from
misty smoke and gases hideous room with a bed touching
each wall dirty soiled bed words on the walls open windows
with faces open mouths watering eyes clawing hands reaching inside Lar twisting and writhing with someone else using
a strap on her, half human, inhuman unfinished human figures unfinished dancing drawing percussion weapons deafening noises of explosions and smells of gunpowder screams
targets chained to trees out of range of their bullets beams
touching them touching them only not lingering only touching them out of range of their bullets out of range of their
bullets. . . . Brunce's gun in his hand spreading circle of
blood on the shoulder of Gene Connors Brunce's eyes boring
into his the smoking revolver in his hand still behind Gene
behind Trace. . . . Running past Gene's body. . . . You've
been to Tarbo boy! You've been to Tarbo totarbototarbo . . .
don't want to kill them you don't want not to. Indifference
is worse than sheer brutality Captain Tracy. They are people
like you like me like the Outsiders.

Trace was sitting where he had dropped, still clad in his
all-weather suit, one arm dangling, the other stretched out
on the maps, both numbed and asleep. The stool on which
he sat was small, plastic, and he could no longer feel it
under him, nor could he feel his feet and legs held too long
in one position. His face mask and helmet protected his face
from the surface of the pull-down desk top, and with any
slight shift of his position he felt that he was floating, as he
was, surrounded by foam and the ungiving rigidity of the
helmet and face piece. He had turned off the audio and the
helmet was soundproof without it. He had forgotten to turn
on the night glow inside the dinghy and without it there
was a complete absence of light. He had no sense of touch,
of heat, cold, sound, sight . . . no sensory data of any kind,
only a mind, free-floating, unattached.

Before his open, straining eyes paraded images superimposed one on another until there was no interior quiet; in his inner ear voices were raised and lowered. He could not tell if it lasted for minutes or hours; he could not tell if he felt the sensations he experienced in his mind only or in mind and body. When the figures were threatening, sometimes he ran, feeling hot and flushed with the effort, feeling the strain in his leg muscles and in his chest. His body told him he was running and he believed it. Lights began to come and go, patterned lights, blocks of yellows, with smaller rectangles of red and green or violet and orange . . . lights that grew from coin size to cover the entire field of his vision, lights of dazzling brightness, other lights that were so dim that he squinted in order to see them better. There was a meaning in the lights, if he could only decipher it. The lights lost their precise forms and began wavering, looking like flames, tongues of color that leaped, rose, fell, grew again. He understood that the lights represented his life: they had started subdued and dim without form and had become more and more violent, with rigid shapes, but now again they were formless. To his horror he saw that the clarity of the colors was diminishing; they were becoming muddied and ugly, and he realized that they were blending, all coming together, getting darker, muddier, uglier. He screamed at them to go away. He screamed again and again, for he could not hear the screams that were echoing through the dinghy. The colors ran together and began dripping away from the framework that had held them together. They ran down to form a puddle of colorless muck, and from it rose ship after ship. Outsiders' ships of gold.

They were beautiful ships, slender, long, brilliant, shimmering behind force screens that softened them in outline, made them dreamlike. The Outsiders were tall and slender also, and lovely. He saw them as forms, beautiful forms, with graceful lines and pleasing colors. When he attached the word *outsider* to them the forms changed, and they were no longer human, but masked creatures whose hideousness was hidden. He could hear them speaking: we don't want war; we don't want to harm anyone; you must return to your homelands and venture forth no more until you are welcomed to the other worlds, until you have put aside your armaments, until you have replaced your generals with men of peace. . . . He saw them above him. He was on a flight of stairs that wound upward into the sky, and slightly to one side, and above him, was Lar; above both of them stood the glorious Outsiders, inhuman, more than human, beautiful. He hadn't known the stairs continued above him; no one ever told him to look upward to see; he never had been able to see up that high before. He could hear Lar's bit of poetry in his ear as he gazed up at the tall figure above him:

> Without ever new evil, how know good?
> In a world without ugliness, is there beauty?

He stood paralyzed on the stair and the Outsider was changing even as he gazed. It was taking on a metallic look, growing outward, getting rounder, with a single red eye in the middle of its head, a head that had grown domelike. The red eye began searching for him. He knew it was searching for him, that it would not be satisfied with anything else. He reached his foot out behind him, feeling for the stairs he had climbed before. They were gone; only charred remains of them jutted from the framework of the staircase. He looked back and knew that to step backward was to die. It was more than miles down, an eternity of falling, an infinity of space lay behind him, more than could be covered in a lifetime. He stood on the narrow step and looked again at the robot turning its single eye to the right and left, searching for him. He knew it would find him this time. As the eye passed over the stairs above him, they vanished. Presently there were no other steps, only the one on which he continued to stand and it was alone and unsupported now. The one piece of wood floating alone.

"Who trained you?" he shouted at the robot then, and faintly, like an echo, Lar's voice answered, "Trained to be a soldier, trained to be a soldier, trained. . . ." He looked behind him, and he knew he could not go back. He could not return by the steps he had already used, and there was no other way. There was no way back or out for him, only death when the red eye found him, when the two of them finally met, each built for this one thing, each performing as he must in this one encounter. The buttons had all been pushed, and now there was only the response to them left to the two who soon must stare face to face.

He had his Tarbo; the robot had his Tensor. Neither of them could erase what had been built in. . . . The red eye turned and turned, and it would fall on him soon. Eternities passed, and he had to do something. He screamed and flailed his arms and legs. He could not feel them, could not know if they moved, knew only that consciously he tried to swing his arms about, tried to kick out with his feet. One hand brushed against the switch that activated the audio of his helmet, and he could hear his own screams, and with the sound it was as if he were released from a spell. His groping, clawing hands found switches in the dinghy and there was light. Still the hoarse voice screamed until finally the screams gave way to sobbing, and sobbing he yanked off the suit and flung it from him.

Something had happened to him and he could not tell what it had been. He could not think, could only shiver with dread. He knew that, if he had stayed in the suit, out of touch with physical reality, he would have died. His mind would have given in to the hallucinatory images and he would have died, probably screaming until the end. He shivered again, harder, shaking uncontrollably.

He staggered across the dinghy to take a sip of water. It would be gone before noon. There had been images that he had to think about, clear from his mind once and for all, or risk insanity. He couldn't think of them yet, and he knew he could not. He wrote them down in a shaky script: Lar and aliens Tarbo Duncan's death the Outsiders. . . . Then he returned to his seat-bed and stretched out and immediately fell asleep.

Sixteen

Trace awakened slowly, painfully. He didn't want to wake up again. He wanted to return to the void that sleep had brought this time, a void with no thoughts, no pains, no thirst. A groan escaped his lips when he moved and slowly he dragged himself from the seat-bed and stood up. He looked down at himself with disgust and loathing. His body was filthy with sweat, dust, sand, dried blood. . . . He was gaunt and bony. Fever, work, heat and worry had carved away his flesh until little was left but leatherlike skin stretched over sharp bones.

He knew he was feverish that morning, probably had been slightly feverish ever since arriving in this hell. Thank god for the antifever capsules. There was a tic on the side of his face when he reached for a tube of the food, and he felt a wave of nausea pass through him. He had to take it; it contained some moisture and his water was down to less than a cupful. He took out the water bag and stared at it regretfully: less than half a cup. He sat down, with half of the water and a tube of fruit mixture and two of the antifever capsules. His mouth felt caked inside, hard and sore, with deep cracks on the outside. His tongue was swollen, filling his entire mouth. He touched water to his tongue, took his time with the first scant spoonful. It hurt his throat. Something had happened to him. He couldn't seem to concentrate on anything long enough to think it through. It took more water to get the capsules down, and his throat burned all the way. At the first taste of the pasty fruit he put it aside. He could not take that now. He looked at it for a long time and finally tried again, this time managing two swallows of it. He finished his water then and could have wept for more.

He had to inspect the passage he had worked on. Without thinking of anything, he got into his suit, left the audio on full this time, left the lights on in the dinghy, and went outside. His feet seemed not to be making contact with the ground as he crossed the valley floor, and he felt that the short trip either took only an instant or was endless. He felt that it was important to decide which, but even as he wondered about it he forgot how he was trying to apply the time scale. When he got to the entrance of the passage he forgot why he was there. He turned to go back to the dinghy, hesitated, and for no real reason went instead into the passageway between the cliffs. A barrier stopped him and he gaped at it with surprise. He couldn't remember it at all. It was made of sand and rocks, was over his head, stretching from one wall to the other. Unsteadily he climbed over a rock or two to get a higher viewpoint, and from there he could see that the barrier appeared to stretch out the rest of the length of the passageway. He remembered working on it then, but dimly, as if that were an incident from ages past, from another lifetime. He decided to rest in the shade of the cliff and he sat down, and again time was meaningless to him.

The medication moved through his system sluggishly; until the stimulants contained in it reached his brain, he sat unmoving in the shade. He sat without thought until, very slowly, patterns started to form again and he knew this was the fifth day, that on the following day he could expect the arrival of the robot. He got up, and when he looked again at the sand and stone barriers he knew they would prevent entry through this passage into his valley. Concentrating on his movements, he left the passage and went to the one that remained. It was even broader, with only two narrow spots in it. It was practically a straight cut most of the way through the granite cliff, fairly steep but not so steep that the robot could not manage it. He followed it to the end, coming to one turn of about 100° after two more gentle curves. The grade at the turn was steeper than it had been both below and above that spot. Trace stared at it for several seconds, turned and studied the passage behind him, and then clambered up to the top and outside. He examined the passage from the top. He could see that it went down into the valley, although he couldn't see past the turn. The robot would know this was an entrance. If he could block it there where it curved . . .

Whatever he planned to do, he knew he had to do it that morning and afternoon. Time was running out on him, and there was the problem of the recurring fever attacks. But what difference if he did block it from the valley? It could only be temporary. Once it knew that he was in the valley, the robot could get in. His pitiful barricade would bar it no more than a wall of loosely stacked children's blocks would bar an adult from a room. He slumped to the ground again and looked out at the world beyond his valley. The sun was nearly overhead already, but would not reach into the passage for half an hour or longer, would not shine directly into it longer than another half hour before the other wall provided shade again. He could remain in it working . . . "For what?" His voice was a croak, hoarse from dryness, from screaming in the night hours. His throat rasped and hurt when he spoke. There had been the slight chance that he might find the other dinghy in the five or six days that he had gained by returning to this end of the mountains. The gamble had been lost. The robot was able to control the screen from a distance. He knew he could not enter the dinghy as long as the screen was effective. If he could trap the robot, force it to turn off the screen . . . he laughed wildly. The laughter stopped abruptly and he stared again at the passage. Had this been what he had worked for all along without realizing it? He could build a trap, a trap using what he had: wind, sand, rocks, and the natural pitch of the passage.

From where he was at the outer end of the passage he could not see past the turn; from here it appeared that the floor of the passage itself sloped fairly evenly, a little steep, but not dangerously so, until there was a sudden dropping away of the floor over a twenty-foot stretch immediately before the twist in the passage. Seeing the change in grade, he could brace for it, be prepared for it. . . . If it were concealed under loose sand it would make a trap. The passage was heavily strewn with rocks and boulders, both above and below the turn. If the robot were mired in sand there, it might be possible to bombard it with the rocks. It might be damaged by the sand itself, lose its balance and be unable to rise again.

If it got that close to him he had to have something ready for it, something to slow it down. Otherwise it would enter the valley and kill him and the whole flight and fight would have been for nothing, only a delay of the inevitable. Trace knew he could not give up after fighting so hard. He started to build another wall of rocks.

He brought rocks from the valley floor and one by one hauled them up the passageway and laid them down until he had enough to start piling them. The barrier would have to be four feet high here where it was hidden from the outside by the turn. When the wind blew the sand it would dump it over the fence on the other side, where, hopefully, it would be leveled out and give the impression of being the floor itself. The passage was three hundred feet long and contained many tons of loose rocks and boulders, many more tons of sand. The hours passed; the sun blazed down into the narrow cut between the massive cliffs, and then started to descend, leaving the cut in deep shadow.

Trace worked deliberately, not thinking about the work he was doing, not thinking about the agony of his body as he lifted rocks, staggered with them up the passage and dropped them by the growing wall. He didn't ask himself why he didn't use the rocks nearer at hand, why he returned the 240 feet to the valley floor for his supply each time. The world swam in a red haze before his eyes and he did not find it strange. There were murmurs in his ears, words, phrases, snatches of song and music, and he did not find them incongruent. Somewhere between the valley and the turn in the passage he began speaking; when he opened his mouth to utter the words one of the cracks started to bleed and the trickle of blood oozed from his lip, rolled crookedly down his chin and out of sight down his neck.

"You can't count on the men being able to kill unless they are taught to kill. An early figure given was on the order of 60 per cent who never fired directly at the enemy. . . . The enemy is always the objective, never a man, or a group of men, or a town of people. It's a platoon, or the target, or the objective. You can shoot anything at an objective. An objective doesn't die, it is merely met and taken. You don't hate the enemy, men. You can't afford to hate the enemy because hatred involves the emotions and a man with emotions driving him is not a man to be trusted in war. You all measured up. Those who didn't measure up were mustered out of the army."

He heard the words as if from a great distance, unaware that he was saying them. How do I know they all measured up? he asked, questioning the voice that seemed so unrelated to him.

Because they've all been to Tarbo.

He dropped a rock and stood still for a long time, and he was not seeing the glaring red world of rocks and desert, but the soft misty forests of Tarbo, and he saw all of it. That was where they were sorted. Those who could and did kill from those who couldn't or didn't. Some were assigned to paper work after Tarbo, some were assigned to the fleet. Some of them never left Tarbo. He saw again the smoking revolver in Brunce's hand, saw the spreading blood on Gene Connors' shoulder, in the back. Fishing in stocked waters, Gene had said. He had guessed. Those who knew the truth about Tarbo didn't leave it.

A gust of wind drove a handful of sand against Trace's face mask and he jerked. He shook his head hard and pulled away from the wall of the passage that was supporting him. He didn't know how long he had been leaning against it. He could see into the valley; it was striped black and white with phantom sand figures rising, swirling, falling. Without looking at the wall he had been building, he left the passage and crossed the valley floor, his head bowed against the driving sand and wind, his shoulders slumped in defeat. He knew the heat and wind and sand were beating him after all. He didn't care any longer. Inside his dinghy he pulled off his suit and fell down on the seat-bed. There was no water; he could swallow none of the tubed food without water. He could not even take any more of the antifever capsules. He could only wait, and hope for sleep.

You're army, Trace. Forget her.

"Shut up, Duncan! I wanted you to stay with me and you wouldn't, now just shut up!"

We need the reinforcement of others of our own kind, trained men as we have been trained, murderers, just as we are murderers. Or else we might start to think.

Can't have that, old man. Just do, never think.

Who said that? His father? He stared wildly about the

dinghy. What was his father doing in it? He hadn't seen him since . . . when? He didn't know. Seventh birthday? Sixth?

A convenience, dear, that's all.

They were gone. He turned to the other seat-bed and said in his croaking voice, "I tried to save you, Duncan, you know that."

But only because you were afraid to be alone, Trace. Afraid to think . . .

"You went there too, Duncan. We all did. Part of the training. We weren't responsible for it."

Sure, Trace. Sure. Forget it. Forget her. Not human, even. You know what they're good for.

There was no letup. His body twitched now and then and the only sounds that he made were groans and indecipherable mutterings, but there was no quiet. The winds howled through the valley and he didn't hear them.

On the other side of the valley the wind hurled tons of sand through the passageway. Much of it was blown straight through, high over the meager wall of stone. Some of it was caught by the wall, and in turn served as a trap for more of the sand. A mound of it grew. When the wind passed its most furious peak and became gentle again, the top of the mound was leveled. The black, still night settled over the planet, but there was no quiet in the dinghy until exhaustion dragged Trace from the clamoring voices, shutting them out finally so he could sleep. It was dawn, and in the dawn the winds returned. Sand was added to the accumulation in the passage, mounded again, this time ten feet high, and then leveled once more, and the new level was only seven feet, flush with the ground beyond the passage at the far end of it, the end through which the robot would try to gain entry.

The sound of the radiation alarm woke Trace. It was coming! His eyes were bright with fever and his hand trembled when he adjusted the screen to focus in on the target. It was still four miles from him, but coming steadily. His mouth was partially open; he couldn't close it. He touched his tongue and found it hot and dry, swollen. He was dying. Shaking violently, he started the engines of the dinghy. He would die, but not under the beam of the laser, not from the robot. He eased the dinghy to the mouth of the chimney and stopped it again, without turning off the engine immediately. He would wait until the robot started to enter the valley, and then he would leave, go as far as his fuel would take him, and die alone. He felt eager to be off, to get started on that, his last retreat.

He watched its progress on his screen, sometimes seeing it singly, sometimes seeing an infinite regression of screens, each with the moving speck of light, stretching out endlessly before him, and he waited. He shook now and again, heaving spasms that left him gasping. "Come on," he coaxed it. "Come on!" It circled the valley, like a sniffing dog circling a lake to find where its quarry had entered the water. It found the blocked passage and tried it, and was turned back by the sand that filled the narrow cut from wall to wall. It continued its circle. It came to the next passage and hesitated a second. Trace saw the passage through its eyes then: an apparent floor that was fairly level, dotted with rocks and boulders, no different from the rest of the hellish terrain.

It rolled into the passage, its wheels finding traction on the rock base covered with sand. The dot of light moved on the screen. Trace drew in a long, painful breath and held it.

The robot moved slowly; having learned that one passage was blocked, it was alert for blockage in this one. Behind it the sand was flattened, small rocks were crushed, glinting new cuts to the sun. Nothing was there to be seen except the trail of crushed rocks and packed sand. The trail grew longer, at a maddeningly slow pace. The sand under its wheels deepened somewhat and it stopped again. It moved forward once more, using the treads now. The sound of rocks being ground to powder was the only sound to be heard. It was as if a shadow passed over the ground, and when it moved on there was new sand where there had been rocks. From both sides of the trail it made, sand trickled in to fill the depressions its treads left. It was unbalanced by the abrupt drop concealed with sand, and for a moment it hung, braking, but under the treads the slithery sand shifted and it was further unbalanced. Behind it, where sand trickled into one of the ruts it had left, a rounded rock followed the sand and gravity pulled it, keeping it in the smooth track. It hit the robot from behind, lodging under the tread. Another rock followed, and then another. The robot hung, unmoving then; its eight ton body against the unsettled sand proved too much, and it slipped four feet before it could make an effort to stop itself. The sudden surge of its weight on the sand pressing against the loosely piled rock wall was more than the wall could bear. It gave way and there was a crash of rocks and sand pouring through the break, as water pours through a broken dam. The robot toppled when the sand shifted from under it. With a thunderous crash it hit the ground where the grade was steepest. It rolled, and over and around it fell an avalanche of rocks and sand, sweeping up everything in its path. Rocks struck the walls, were dashed back, hit the robot's screen and penetrated it. The force shield protected it from high-energy impact of any sort, but the rocks were of low-energy yield and they hit the robot, as did the sand. In the first ten seconds after its fall the screen controls and the remote control for the dinghy's screen were inactivated; in the next ten seconds one of the flexible, handlike waldoes was torn loose. It withdrew all other appendages and closed all its apertures, but sand had entered and damage was done.

The crashing fall and roll of the massive robot tore loose boulders from the cliffs themselves. Rocks that the wind had deposited in the passage were loosened and tumbled after the robot. When it stopped rolling it was under a mountain, twenty-five to thirty tons of sand, another thirty-five to fifty tons of rocks and boulders.

Trace stared at the hill of rocks and sand, awed by what he had done. As he watched, the hill stirred, shifted, a rock rolled down from it, then several more, and a spot of brightness appeared near the top. The robot's laser was still working. It was burning its way out.

It reminded Trace of a nightmare in which no matter how far or how fast he ran, every time he looked over his shoulder the devil was still there, the same distance, still grinning in anticipation. He watched the red spot until it vanished. The laser had cut through. The robot would widen the opening, dislodging or burning rocks to free itself, and then they would be back where they had started. He watched, but the hole didn't grow. The robot couldn't move. The laser happened to be pointing in that direction when it was turned on, but it could not direct the beam to another spot. Trace laughed. His lips cracked more and bled, and it hurt his throat, but he laughed until he was weak and the laughter had turned to sobbing. It passed and he looked again at the hole made by the laser. It had grown slightly. Perhaps it had a range of freedom of an inch or so, back and forth one inch, or two at the most. He took off then in the dinghy as the stabbing laser bit another eighth of an inch away. The top opening grew to almost two inches in length.

Trace landed on the cliff over the passage, and cautiously he eased to the edge to look down on the mountain that was the robot's burial mound. The cherry glow showed first on one end of the two-inch cut, then on the other. Trace backed away and looked about him. The top of the cliff was covered with stones, rocks from pea size to boulders as big as houses. He grinned and cried out with pain when his lip split further. Water. He could find the dinghy now, with the screen turned off, and then he would finish burying the robot.

He almost crashed his dinghy when he landed only twenty feet from the other one, now out in the open and visible. He was crying deep in his throat when his trembling hands opened the emergency stores unit and found the water bags there. Enough water to last him for a month, two months. He drank deeply and in a minute he was sick, vomiting all of it up again. He sipped a mouthful then and let it trickle down. His throat was swollen almost shut. He was shivering uncontrollably. Much of the water ran down his chin, ran out of his stiff mouth, spilled even before he could get it near his lips. This time the small amount he allowed himself stayed down, and he took another mouthful, and then another.

After he had drunk he loaded the water and the fuel from the robot's dinghy into his own, and then he returned to the cliff and the robot. He had to stay near it, keep it covered. When the winds started he would return to his chimney and stay there in the shelter. During the night, when the wind was gone, he would light the robot with his spotlights, keep it covered at all times. During the day he would stay on the cliff and it would keep him busy just finding stones he could roll to the edge and push over. He worried about keeping it all done. It was a two-man job, and he was alone. It did not occur to him to leave now, to return to his orbiting ship and wait there for relief. He had trapped it, and he would hold it for them, would direct their fusion bombs to it himself. He looked down at it and saw that the hole was three inches long, first one end of the line turning red, then the other end, as the laser swept back and forth steadily, without pause.

Seventeen

Trace pushed rocks over the edge of the cliff; he shoved over all that were within reach. Some of them vaporized in air, vanishing with a cloud that quickly dispersed, others hit resoundingly, now and then upsetting the balance of the artificial hill, dislodging more than they added. When the wind blew too hard for him to continue on the top of the cliff he returned to his chimney. He drank deeply and washed himself, and then he ate; he even made coffee. He found an ointment and applied it to his lips. When the winds died down he left the chimney, landed the dinghy in the valley where he could floodlight the pile of rocks and sand and study it for any change. Almost immediately a red glow showed, not at the top this time, but three fourths of the way up, in the side that faced the valley. The robot had been able to shift its position. The wind had driven sand over it, piling it higher on the far side, but thinning the nearer side somewhat.

Trace worked on adding rocks to the pile until the morning wind drove him back to the chimney. He was exhausted, trembling with fatigue when he turned off the engine.

It doesn't end, Duncan. Goes on and on . . .

A logic box, Trace, that's all, a logic box.

On and on, automatically, without thought, without heart, without pain.

You have no heart, Captain Tracy, no thought for those who live on the worlds you take, no pain for those who bleed.

Logic box, Trace . . . can't do anything not programmed in, can't think.

As an officer you have to command instant obedience in your men, not because they agree, or like your plan, or because of anything except that you pushed the buttons that put them in motion. Do you men understand that? Instant obedience. All the way up the line!

Nothingness of sleep then, and waking to fear. How long had he slept? Was it still there? He shook all over until he located it in the visual scanner and saw that it was still covered. Weakly he staggered to the storage unit and prepared food. He would have to set an alarm, not sleep over a couple of hours at a time. He went again to the cliff top and surveyed the hill below. The wind had piled up the rocks and sand higher than ever on the passage side of the robot, but the valley side was being denuded. He turned his detector on the hill and located the robot inside it, less than fifteen feet from the valley side of the mound. The beam was cutting a hole five inches long, not directly up now, but toward the side, back and forth, back and forth, five inches, five and a half, six. . . . Feverishly Trace searched for rocks that he could shove over the edge. The sun climbed through the sky, filled it and turned the world into a dazzling glare of white-hot light. He worked on. He was perspiring profusely; for the first time in days he had enough water to let him sweat. He worked without thought, until suddenly he staggered. The ground was spinning, and the cliffs were rising and falling erratically.

He pitched forward. When he roused, moments later, he had no way of knowing how long he had lain there. He was burning up, dry, and he knew he was suffering from heat prostration. He had to get out of the sun, get his body temperature down, start the flood of sweat again.

He dragged himself to the dinghy and got into it. He had

neglected to take the medicine that morning, he realized, had expected the abundance of water to heal him. He thought of the killer robot fighting as hard as it could to free itself, and a wave of pity passed through him. He sponged his body, caught the water in a plastic sheet to cool again that night, sponged himself over and over.

Afterward he rested on the seat-bed. He could not work out in the sun during the middle of the day. He had to remember that there was too little oxygen in the air to support strenuous effort over any length of time. He had to remember that he was sick, really sick. He wondered if the robot had been programmed to feel its hurts. He hoped not. "It is such a waste," he whispered once. Pain was such a waste.

Later he went back out and stared down at the burial mound. "I'm sorry for you," he said. "None of it is really your fault." He shoved over the rocks he had accumulated there at the edge. Tomorrow he would have to go farther afield to get the rocks to add to the pile. It was time then to get back to the safety of the chimney.

In the days that followed he was building a new world, laboriously adding to the foundations, or raising new walls of incredible beauty. Sometimes he was building a simple house for Lar. Again it was a monument to mankind that he was erecting. It was an edifice that required exquisite care. His selection of his material was meticulous, his handling of the building blocks almost gentle, his concern for the thing under his cornerstone was urgent. He talked to it incessantly, describing the stones he was using, explaining the purpose of the building. Sometimes he merely worked doggedly, refusing to think about the condition of his body, the condition of his mind, hinted at by the great, growing gaps when he could remember nothing at all of what he did or what he thought. The voices were in the dinghy constantly now, remaining there when he left, continuing when he returned. Sometimes it was the voices that directed

him in the preparation of food, or reminded him to take
medicine, or to set the alarm, or to move to the chimney
before the winds came. He would have died without the
voices leading him through the bad hours. He selected the
rocks he would use with infinite patience, rejecting those
that were too jagged, feeling happiness when he came
across one of particularly pleasing shape or color. These he
examined many times before pushing them over the side.
He would tell it about the rocks he was sending to it. His
voice was low and kind when he spoke to it.

He talked to it of the Outsiders. "They will push us back
to the three worlds of the Solar System," he said. "Then
we'll have to learn many new things, how to live on only
three worlds, how to use the land we'll have then. It won't
be easy. But we can't fight them, you know." He spoke to it
about Lar, about Duncan, about death and life. It never
answered him. The sweep of its laser was the only sign
that it still lived. He began waiting for the beam to reach
the wall of the cliff before he went on after telling it something new. When it touched the side of the cliff and started
back toward the other side it was his signal that he was
to continue. Back and forth, from one side of the passage
to the other, sixteen feet here at the entrance.

He felt particularly pleased with it when it made some
unexpected gain, clearing more of the rubble from itself
than he had anticipated, freeing one of its sensors, or widen-
ing the range of its beam. Almost regretfully he would push
the rocks over the edge then, as if ashamed to continue in
the face of such courage.

He asked the voices if it actually possessed courage, and
they debated the answer for days without coming to a decision. Then his radio hummed and the panel light went on
and he knew the relief ship was within radio range. When
his report was given and the radio went silent he found that
tears were on his cheeks, the sound of a voice that was not

inside his head had released the hysteria that had been accumulating for a month. He went outside to the edge of the cliff and shouted at the robot.

"It's over now, brother! They'll be here in a few hours and then you'll be finished for good! Do you know what I'm saying to you?"

He waited until the beam bit into the side of the crevice wall and started to swing back toward the other side, and he nodded. It knew. It wouldn't matter now if it did get loose. They could find it and drop bombs on it wherever it went. Again it was the hunted, no longer the hunter. He laughed his relief. He didn't push any more rocks over the edge. Let it struggle.

He went back inside and bathed. He ate and then policed up the dinghy. He even washed the all-weather suit. He had the relief ship on the radar screen and he sat watching its approach with satisfaction. Twice he went back to the cliff and looked down at the robot, measuring its progress. As he watched, the pile of loose rocks and sand shifted, rocks tumbling and rolling away from the hill. It was frantic, he knew, just as he had been frantic waiting for its arrival. He said softly, "I am sorry, brother. You fought a good fight all the way."

For the first time, there was no overtone of fear and hatred in his voice when he addressed it. It had always done exactly what it had been designed to do, no more, certainly no less than that. The radio beep recalled him to the dinghy.

"Captain Tracy, this is General MacClure speaking. Congratulations, Trace. You've done a magnificent job down there. You'll be rewarded handsomely you can be sure of that. You name it, boy, whatever you want. We have aboard an army scientist, Trace. Colonel Langtree. Answer his questions, Captain Tracy."

"Yes sir," Trace said, bewildered. He had heard once that

Langtree had been one of the scientists who let the robot get away from Venus. He waited. Presently the thinner, more petulant voice of the scientist was in his ears.

"Captain, you say the robot is not destroyed? Is that right?"

"Yes sir, that is correct."

"To what extent is it damaged?"

For the next half hour Trace answered the scientist's questions, describing in detail the pursuit over the mountains, the activities of the robot since its entrapment, the abilities he had been able to observe while it was still free. There was silence for five minutes after the questioning, and then MacClure was back.

"Trace, you are going to be picked up and brought aboard. We will give rendezvous coordinates immediately after this communication. Now, tell me this, is the robot within radio range?"

"Yes sir. The dinghy is within a hundred and fifty feet of it."

"Good. Turn your receiver on loud, so that it can hear. We want it, Trace. The Outsiders won't negotiate worth a damn. The one ultimatum was it, with no area for negotiations. They insist that we withdraw back to the Solar System to be kept there in quarantine until we meet their requirements to qualify us as legitimate space travelers. It will be death to the World Group. We can't fight them now, but if we have that robot, learn how it has developed that screen and adapt it to our ships . . . build more robots with that shield. . . . We'll take the entire galaxy, Trace, Outsiders and all. They don't have anything that can compare to that invisibility shield. We need the robot. You're going to be the biggest hero since Prometheus, Trace."

What MacClure had said was true, Trace would be the biggest hero in the galaxy; it was in MacClure's voice when he spoke to him, a note of deference already. The note would echo, would boom. This then was what the forty days

had been for. Trace laughed in exultation and turned up
the radio so that the robot could hear. He went outside to
watch it, to hear with it the words coming from the ship.
A three-foot segment of the cliff edge had been vaporized
in a precise semicircular pattern. Trace stayed away from
that area. Langtree's voice sounded loud and close.

"You, Dr. Vianti's robot, this is Colonel Langtree speaking
to you. I know you can hear me and understand my words.
I have a message for you. You understand about destruction
and death. You understand about preserving your own life.
You are trapped and doomed to destruction now. You know
that we can drop bombs on you from miles above you, out
of reach of your laser. You have seen these bombs. You
learned about them back on Venus. Scan your memory banks
and you will know that I did not want your destruction
under the seas of Venus. That was a mistake. We want you
alive and functioning. We want to learn from you, and
we want to provide you with more abilities. We can do this.
You know we can give you more abilities, better abilities.
You must cooperate with us or we will destroy you."

Trace's eyes followed the trail of the laser, no longer
sweeping back and forth in a straight line, but wobbling,
making a figure eight that was growing wider, burning into
a larger area of the cliff as he watched. It would be free in
an hour or so. As soon as it was able to burn a round hole
it would start enlarging it until it was free. The voice was
continuing over the radio.

"If you understand my words you know that what I have
said is true. You have been programmed to preserve yourself. Now you must follow my orders or you will allow yourself to be destroyed. You must turn off the laser."

The beam vanished.

Trace hadn't believed it could happen, hadn't believed the
robot capable of understanding to this degree. Suddenly the
fear that had left him returned heavier than before. He

backed from the edge of the cliff and went inside the dinghy. MacClure was speaking to him, ordering him to adjust the radio so that the robot couldn't hear them. Trace made his report of the robot's response to Langtree's offer and he heard the triumphant note in MacClure's voice. Trace was given coordinates for pickup, and the radio became silent. He stared at it.

They didn't know what they were doing.

He remembered the other dinghy, equipped with the screen, and he started his engine. He had to go to the rendezvous point. He would go there and wait. He didn't want to wait with the killer robot. His fever was high; he had ignored it in the excitement of the arrival of the relief ship. The ship was going into orbit now, he noted. They would dispatch the pickup craft within minutes. In half an hour it would be on the planet; he would get in, and they would take care of him. A long rest, vacation, they would get Lar for him, bring her to him wherever he said. He could retire now, a rich man, with everything a man could want for the rest of his life.

A disease spreading through the galaxy . . .

Like a virus that could not be seen, that was deadly and swift, they would move through the galaxy, world by world falling before them, under the fire of their robots, both metal and flesh. . . . He took off, swinging north, and landed near the other dinghy. He turned off his radiation detector, but the voices remained with him, louder, insistent, each clamoring for attention. He couldn't turn them off. He tried to ignore them as he worked inside the other dinghy. Then he turned again to his own dinghy and left the spot. The rescue craft was on the radar screen, but he didn't look at it. The radio was buzzing angrily at him, someone wanting to know what he had done, where he had gone and why.

For the first time since he was twelve he ignored the voice of a superior officer, didn't even hear the voice over the other voices that were louder, more insistent.

He thought of Venus, his birthplace, swamps and soft forests, steam and mud, and he knew he loved it. He thought of Mars, hard, cold air, domed cities, a vast frigid desert. He thought of Earth, overflowing with life, polluting its seas, lakes, rivers, forests, careless and indifferent because there were so many more worlds out there. Something Lar once said, and he hadn't understood: "Drink first yourself of the cup you would offer a stranger." Indifferent, happy-go-lucky Earthman, not responsible for the cup proffered the stranger; let him now drink of it himself.

Behind him a fountain of rubble erupted as the igniter he had rigged touched off the fuel that he had turned into a bomb. The other dinghy was gone. Trace was well schooled in the art of demolition. He didn't turn back to check the damage; he knew that it would be complete destruction, that no part would remain in sufficient quantity to be reassembled for study.

The dinghy skimmed close to the ground. There was the cottony sky overhead, with a glare that half filled it. There were the white cliffs and the black cliffs, and beyond them the white wool desert, interwoven with silver threads in a random pattern, where sky and land met like the inside of a flattened sphere. There were the gentle hills stretching endlessly as the winds tore down the mountains and deposited them grain by grain on the dunes. One day it would be a world of nothing but desert, a world of death and heat and glaring white desolation. It was like Tarbo, Trace thought. Once you understand it, you don't leave it.

He circled the valley, gained altitude and speed and circled it again. He could see a small section of the robot where it had freed itself from the mountain of rocks and sand. It was a brilliant reflection that pained his eyes. He locked in on the robot then and when he turned the last time there was no way he could change his mind, no way he could stop. He felt nothing. He had known that he had to find the killer robot and destroy it. He had found two. . . . "The war's over for both of us, brother," he murmured. When the killer things met in a fiery embrace the voices were singing.